FOUR ROMANTIC TALES
from 19th Century German

FOUR
ROMANTIC
TALES

from 19th Century German

Translated, with an Introduction, by
HELENE SCHER

Frederick Ungar Publishing Co.
New York

Translated from the German: *Der blonde Eckbert/* Tieck; *Geschichte vom braven Kasperl und dem schönen Annerl*/Brentano; *Der tolle Invalide auf dem Fort Ratonneau*/Arnim; *Des Vetters Eckfenster*/Hoffmann.

Copyright © 1975 by Frederick Ungar Publishing Co., Inc.

Printed in the United States of America

Designed by Irving Perkins

ISBN 0-8044-2010-6 (cloth)

ISBN 0-8044-6005-1 (paper)

Library of Congress Cataloging in Publication Data

Scher, Helene, comp.
    Four romantic tales from 19th century German.

    CONTENTS: Tieck, L. Blond Eckbert.—Brentano, C. The story of Honest Casper and Fair Annie.—Arnim, A. von. The mad invalid of Fort Ratonneau. [etc.]
    1. Short stories, German—Translations into English. 2. Short stories, English—Translations from German. 3. German fiction—19th century—Translations into English. 4. English fiction—Translations from German. I. Title.
PZ1.S2876Fo   [PT1327]   833'.01   75-1428
ISBN 0-8044-2769-0
ISBN 0-8044-6304-4 pbk.

Contents

Introduction

IN the last years of the eighteenth century, a group of young writers and philosophers decided to gather regularly for good conversation and fellowship in the German university town of Jena, soon making it a center of intellectual ferment. Enthusiastically, and sometimes to all hours of the night, they discussed and criticized one another's innovative ideas and nascent literary ventures; and their short-lived journal *Athenäum* (1798-1800) was to have an almost revolutionary impact among the intellectuals of Europe. The members of this circle came to be regarded as the Jena Romantics and included the brothers August Wilhelm and Friedrich Schlegel, both eminent critics and literary theorists, the poets Ludwig Tieck, Novalis, and Clemens Brentano, and the philosophers Fichte, Schleiermacher, and Schelling.

Although the group soon disbanded, the speculative essays, criticism, aphorisms, and literary works it produced were to define the concerns and aesthetic attitudes for several generations of Romantic writers, in Germany as well as elsewhere in Europe. On the basis of the theoretical framework evolved by the Jena group, after about 1805 German Romantic writers embarked upon a more practical and enormously creative phase: Brentano, Achim von Arnim, Adalbert von Chamisso, Joseph von Eichendorff, Heinrich von Kleist, and E.T.A. Hoffmann conceived most of the literary masterpieces of German Romanticism, Brentano and Arnim collected German folk songs, and the brothers Jakob and Wilhelm Grimm studied German folklore and the national past, published their famous collection of fairy tales, and founded German philology.

"Romanticism" and "romantic" are problematic terms. Everyone understands, of course, the amorous associations or sentimental mood evoked by the popular colloquial exclamation "How romantic!" As a literary term, however, "romantic" has always been troublesome and ambiguous. Originally designating the qualities characteristic of medieval romance and applied pejoratively during the Age of Reason to anything opposed to a sober, rational view of life, "romantic" gradually acquired positive connotations until the Jena Romantics employed it to describe the highest level of artistic achievement. But neither writers nor critics have ever been consistent in their use of the term. Here are a few of the many definitions typical of the terminological chaos:

"Romanticism is disease, Classicism is health." (Goethe)

"Romantic is that which depicts a sentimental theme in imaginative form." (Friedrich Schlegel)

"The world must be made romantic. Then once more we shall discover its original meaning. To make something romantic is nothing else but a qualitative potentialization. . . Insofar as I render a higher meaning to what is ordinary, a mysterious appearance to what is customary, an infinite look to the finite, I am romanticizing." (Novalis)

"A liberation of the less conscious levels of the mind; an intoxicating dreaming." (F.L. Lucas)

"The addition of strangeness to beauty." (Walter Pater)

"The solitude and enchantment of the forest, the rushing mill-stream, the nocturnal stillness of the German village, the cry of the night watchman, splashing fountains, palace ruins and a neglected garden in which weatherbeaten statues crumble, the fragments of a demolished fortress: everything that creates the yearning to escape from the monotony of daily life is romantic." (Oskar Walzel)

"Romanticism" as a period concept is only slightly less confusing. There remains little doubt that from the last decade of the eighteenth century until the middle of the nineteenth, a spiritual and intellectual movement flourished throughout Europe which distinctly differed from the preceding Age of Reason and from what prevailed after around 1850. But, although many of the impulses and intellectual sources were shared, there was great variation from country to country and from writer to writer. While the restlessness of Romantic writers helped ideas cross national boundaries, individuals set their own accents. Nevertheless, certain common literary concerns can be recognized.

A schematic listing of characteristic Romantic features may help to gain perspective:

1. Cultivation of sensibility, emotions and desires, in opposition to the rationality and common sense proclaimed by the Enlightenment. Emphasis on the irrational, on extremes of subjectivity or introversion, sometimes culminating in melancholy, insanity, or suicide.

2. A quest for wonders: fascination with the mysterious, the fantastic, the magical and the supernatural, but

also with manifestations of the subconscious, dreams, hypnotism, somnambulism, clairvoyance, madness.

3. The cult of nature as a revolt against the artificiality of eighteenth-century urban life. Man's search for harmony in pristine nature, often in the form of ecstatic pantheism.

4. Interest in simple, primitive society, in the "noble savage" uncorrupted by civilization. An almost mystical regard for the "folk soul," especially in Germany, encouraging folkloristic studies and literary genres derived from folk literature, such as fairy tales, legends, folk songs, hymns, and popular plays.

5. Adoration of the Middle Ages, the historical era most intimately associated with romance, leading to nationalism, historicism, and much nostalgia.

6. Contempt for the bourgeois or philistine life style within the narrow confines of rationalistic society, and acclaim for the exceptional man, the genius, the tragic hero, the creative artist or poet.

7. Revival of religious beliefs, longing for the infinite and metaphysical, a search for new myths.

8. Insistence on the primacy of the imagination, resulting in a major reorientation of aesthetic standards and literary methods: absolute rejection of neoclassical rules, preference for unstructured genres such as the novel, and the experimental mixing of genres or of music, literature and the other arts.

The lives and fortunes of the four German writers represented in this volume bear witness to the restlessness and inner conflicts characteristic of Romanticism. Ludwig Tieck (1773-1853) possessed such spectacular writing facility that his numerous works tended to be superficial and unstruc-

tured. Although he was considered a great writer by his con-
temporaries, only his early *Volksmärchen*, the best of which
is *Blond Eckbert*, and some of his parodistic comedies have
stood the test of time. Tieck made his most lasting contribu-
tion to Romanticism as a mediator: he edited the works of
Wackenroder, Novalis, and Kleist, translated Cervantes and
others, completed the pioneering translation of Shakespeare
into German begun by August Wilhelm Schlegel, and gave
famous dramatic recitations of Romantic works. Clemens
Brentano (1778-1842) and Achim von Arnim (1781-1831)
were close friends, in spite of their very different personali-
ties. Brentano, an overly sensitive, dreamy, unstable individual
torn between extremes of mood, interest and goal, was one of
the most important lyric poets of German Romanticism and
also wrote stories, fairy tales, plays, and chaotic novels. In
1817, the year in which he conceived his best shorter narrative, *The Story of Honest Casper and Fair Annie,* Brentano
converted to Catholicism. Subsequently revealing a tendency
toward religious fanaticism, he later spent five years recording
the visions of a stigmatized nun. In contrast to Brentano,
Arnim was a stable, practical man of the world, who studied
the natural sciences before turning to literature. Together
with Brentano he published the important collection of folk
songs, *Des Knaben Wunderhorn,* 1806 and 1808 (*The Boy's
Magic Horn*). True to his scientific inclinations, even his
most fanciful tales are firmly rooted in reality. Ernst Theodor
Amadeus Hoffmann (1776-1822) was the most prolific and
perhaps most gifted of all German Romantic storytellers. He
was a man of many interests and talents; a lawyer by profession, he excelled as a writer, musician (composer and con-
ductor), music critic, painter, caricaturist, stage designer, and
theater director. By the time of his early death from spinal
paralysis, his reputation was well established; and his scurri-

lously humorous and grotesque prose works exerted a power-
ful influence on many later writers, especially on Poe, Musset,
Baudelaire, Gogol, Pushkin, Dostoevsky and Kafka.

The four tales chosen for this anthology illustrate the wide
range of Romantic storytelling, its impressive variety in narrative structure, style, and poetic concerns. Especially characteristic in these tales is the attempt to transcend the limits of
traditional narration through ingenious poetic strategies: by
recourse to the fairy tale (Tieck), by presenting two separate
narratives within a frame which ultimately dominates and by
intermixing poetry and prose (Brentano), or even by doing
away with a conventional plot and presenting instead a series
of loosely interwoven episodes and aphoristic insights in the
form of a conversational arabesque (Hoffmann). Only the
Arnim story adheres to the relatively strict structural require-
ments of the traditional German novella. In all four narratives, storytelling emerges as an overall theme and concern,
realizing in poetic practice the "romanticization" of the every-
day world demanded by the early Romantic theorists Friedrich Schlegel and Novalis. Indeed, Hoffmann's story may and
perhaps ought to be read as a demonstration of how to trans-
form the banal world by means of the power of the imagination into something aesthetically pleasing. All four works
show both fascination with and fear of the demonic chaos and
the mysteries of life which lie beneath its rational surface,
insisting that the dualism inherent in reality be recognized.

Tieck's *Blond Eckbert* (*Der blonde Eckbert,* 1797) is a
highly artistic fairy tale (*Kunstmärchen*), a genre derived
from folk literature that appealed to the Romantics in their
quest for simplicity, uncorrupted nature, the mysterious, and
for an opportunity to give free rein to the imagination. The
characters are only briefly sketched, the place and time of the

action are not made specific, and all sorts of standard fairy tale motifs appear: a castle, forest, trees, rocky crags, a waterfall, a talking bird, and even what appears to be a witch. But in spite of its deceptively simple texture, Tieck's story proves to be a highly complex and ambiguous narrative of mystery and truth, crime and punishment. As more and more levels of guilt are revealed beneath the surface of the seemingly so tranquil life of Bertha and Eckbert, the reader becomes increasingly enthralled by the events culminating in Eckbert's terrifying final moment of truth.

The central episode, Bertha's story of her youth, relates the child's flight from a hostile reality into the fairy tale world of her dreams and her growing up under the protection of magic. Arriving in the supernatural realm of forest solitude only after she undergoes the terrors of total isolation, Bertha experiences the appearance of the initially frightening and sinister old woman with great relief, and she soon learns, through familiarity, to accept the magical world of the forest as both real and truly idyllic. But she cannot remain forever in this childhood paradise of security and innocence, for, while the old woman and her forest realm are unchanging and timeless, Bertha grows older and becomes curious about the outside world she has left behind. It is her natural longing for human companionship that leads her back to the real world, but she cannot leave the realm of childhood innocence without becoming guilty: ostensibly for practical considerations, but perhaps also in the hope of taking some of her childhood security with her, she steals the bird and the precious stones. Although in the course of the subsequent events she repudiates the supernatural world (and thereby her own childhood) and seems to find happiness in the real world as Eckbert's wife, her theft of the magical bird turns out to be a fatal error. As an adult Bertha no longer accepts the supernatural world and indeed kills the bird when it reminds her of her past, yet her life with Eckbert is based on the wealth from the precious stones. Both she and Eckbert remain strangely disturbed by her past and keep it a carefully guarded secret. When Walther mentions the forgotten name of the little dog, Bertha is shocked into confronting the reality of her childhood and her guilt; the repressed supernatural world intrudes into the real and overwhelms her.

Eckbert, too, lives withdrawn from a past reality he suspects but cannot face. The first lines of the story portray a human being who has closed himself off, both physically and psychologically, from the outside world. Eckbert, like Bertha in her childhood, wishes to find security in seclusion. The basic human desire for companionship and intimacy stands in constant conflict with his need for security and fear of disclosing secrets. When Eckbert himself urges Bertha to tell her story, the full significance of which neither realizes, he sets into motion the chain of events which first causes him to murder those he has confided in but is incapable of trusting and finally leads him to the discovery of his own horrifying secret. Eckbert built for himself and Bertha a false paradise, a shaky island of security in the seclusion of his castle which was bound to crumble; man cannot live in total isolation from society and from his true self (cf. the recurrent phrase "without knowing what he was doing"). Both Eckbert and Bertha have become guilty by refusing to integrate the two realms which every human being by necessity must reconcile: the inner and the outer world, the marvelous and the real, life in isolation and in society. Eckbert's ever increasing inability to distinguish the marvelous from the real ultimately leads him to the fatal confrontation with the old woman, who turns out to be the driving force behind the story, both magical (in the forest) and real (Walther and Hugo), both protective (in Bertha's childhood) and punitive (the end of the story). Thus Tieck's masterful tale creates an image of the world in which the natural and supernatural are inextricably blended in both the physical landscape and the realm of the psychological.

The Story of Honest Casper and Fair Annie (Geschichte vom braven Kasperl und dem schönen Annerl, 1817) is more straightforward in tone and form of narration than *Blond Eckbert*, although it contains not one, but two tales within a tale. Brentano begins with what seems to be a narrative frame: the poet-narrator encounters an old peasant woman, who arouses his curiosity with her strange, dignified manner, and he encourages her with gentle but prodding questions to tell her story. He listens with increasing compassion and agitation until he learns of the imminent execution of Annie, at which point he decides to intervene. The frame now becomes the major narrative line as the poet-narrator himself enters the action and participates in the rather melodramatic events leading to the story's conclusion.

The central relationship between the old peasant woman and the poet-narrator determines the mood of the story and sets its rhythm. Speaking with great tranquillity in the calm of the night, the old woman seems to have endless time; she talks slowly, switching from the past to the future and back to the past, while the exactly recorded passing of the night hours intensifies the narrator's sense of foreboding, until his intervention releases the suspense and a rapid denouement ensues. The contrast between the old woman—with her self-assurance and unbroken faith in God the embodiment of the folk virtues admired by so many Romantics—and the deeply troubled narrator figure, who is acutely aware of the ambiguities and uncertainties of life, reveals Brentano's profound skepticism about the value of his own profession as a writer. The old woman causes the narrator great embarrassment when she asks about his trade; he feels a deep sense of shame that he neither performs any useful function in life nor can offer satisfactory answers to problems of human existence. He eventually redeems himself by attempting through his actions (word *and* deed) to save Annie's life. Ironically enough, it is his words—his recounting the story of Casper and Annie—that are most effective and bring about an act of mercy.

Perhaps too emphatically, Brentano's tale focuses on the concept of honor, which each of the characters interprets differently. Casper's primarily military sense of honor seems to have developed from an exaggerated need for worldly approbation, in compensation for the shame he feels about the sloth of his family. When he discovers the shocking truth about his father and stepbrother, it cannot but destroy him. He is spared an even greater disgrace: the knowledge that his beloved Annie, too, has been ruined by the desire for worldly honor. Unlike the psychological factors motivating Casper, Annie's life has been determined from the start by almost magical powers. Convinced by the ominous incidents in her childhood that she is marked by fate, Annie seeks to better her social position in the name of honor. It seems almost incidental that Count Grossinger uses "certain medicines with magical properties" to gain power over her, but once Annie has been abandoned by her aristocratic lover, she atones for her sin of pride by refusing to name her child's father. With her final act, Annie almost matches the old woman's sense of honor, which is clearly religious and moral. The old woman's unwavering trust in divine justice inspires the poet-narrator to do honor by his own profession: his very act of storytelling persuades others to perform good deeds.

Different levels of speech enhance the contrast between the

old woman's inner strength and pious simplicity and the more enlightened but troubled attitudes of the other characters. While the others express themselves fluently in a sophisticated vocabulary, her speech is simple, halting, and repetitive, abounding in Biblical allusions, archaisms, folk sayings, and elements from folk songs and superstition. Yet, recurrent references to objects of central significance such as rose, coin, wreath, sword, teeth, apron, and veil result in effective integration of the different speech styles and various narrative strands.

Based on a real historical incident during the Seven Years' War (1756-1763), Arnim's brilliantly conceived tale *The Mad Invalid of Fort Ratonneau* (*Der tolle Invalide auf dem Fort Ratonneau*, 1818) is the only narrative in this collection that may be termed a novella in the traditional sense. A distinctive short prose genre particularly cultivated in German literature, the novella has a strict, compact structure, few characters, a bizarre or unusual plot, a central, unifying symbol or symbols, and a dramatic sequence of events culminating in a single climactic situation which represents a turning point in the narrative. While the tales by Tieck, Brentano, and Hoffmann possess some features of the novella, only Arnim's story has the perfectly controlled narrative structure and dramatic compactness characteristic of the novella. The principle of condensation is apparent from the outset as the initial grotesquely humorous episode of the burning wooden leg immediately and irrevocably influences the subsequent events. In the ensuing expository flashback, Rosalie simultaneously sketches the portentous details of her past and wins the commandant's full sympathy. After the deceptively idyllic middle episode, in which Francoeur gains the commandant's trust and moves to the fort, the cataclysmic events of the last and longest segment are triggered by Basset's innocent question about Francoeur's health: the turmoil beneath the surface erupts, and only Rosalie's incredible courage can avoid a catastrophe. The climactic confrontation between Rosalie and Francoeur during which Rosalie braves cannon fire is the turning point of the story.

Arnim generates both humorous effects and dramatic suspense by consistently leaving events open to misinterpretation by his characters. With a profound awareness of the ambiguity of human experience, he maintains several levels of meaning throughout the story and gives only the reader, but none of his characters, the privilege of full insight. Most of Francoeur's eccentricities can undoubtedly be explained in purely medical terms. But psychological factors also play a role, especially in the instance when he completely misunderstands Rosalie's reasons for having visited the aging commandant and tries to assess her fidelity with the bizarre omelet test, which she fails from sheer magnanimity toward her guest. Francoeur's tragic belief that Rosalie has been unfaithful is made all the more poignant by the fact that it is the unshakable strength of her love that finally saves him. Francoeur's blasphemous devil's flag makes a mockery of Rosalie's naive conviction that her husband's madness is caused by the devil. But could it perhaps be the devil's influence that makes Francoeur feel pursued by visions of the black priest and speak of a chimneysweep and black miner struggling free when he is cured? Father Philip's ritual attempts to exorcise the devil in Francoeur offer little more than comic relief. But does not Rosalie, too, exorcise the devil in her own way? Arnim motivates every action, every event with multiple factors, so that physical, psychological, and demonic levels of meaning are sustained throughout.

Arnim's use of fire imagery, especially in the literal and figurative fireworks of the last part of the story, unifies and integrates the various levels of meaning. The fire motif appears in numerous manifestations already in the introductory scene: the fire on the hearth, the olive leaves "half burning, half green . . . like hearts in love," the commandant's preoccupation with fireworks, his burning leg spreading fire to Rosalie's apron. Developed with great consistency, the imagery sequence culminates in the fireworks actually staged by Francoeur, which become a symbol of his brilliance and imaginativeness, but also of his potentially explosive nature and diabolical destructiveness. The conciseness of Arnim's imagery, combining physical properties with the demonic, contributes to the lasting impact of this story.

Translated into English here for the first time, *My Cousin's Corner Window* (*Des Vetters Eckfenster*, 1822) is not typically Hoffmannesque: it lacks both plot and the wildly grotesque flights of fantasy and supernatural terrors for which its author is famous. Yet, the little work's significance for Hoffmann and for Romanticism as a whole cannot be disputed, since it offers an entire aesthetic program in miniature. The story has as its *theme* the art of writing and presents the theoretical considerations as well as a practical demonstration of the creative process as perceived by Hoffmann. Though considerably more skeptical and ambivalent than the earlier Romantic writers about the romanticization of reality, in this narrative Hoffmann interprets the artistic confrontation and transformation of reality in defiance of death as an allegory of life itself.

The story begins with a traditional expository passage characterizing the writer known as "my cousin" and the more prosaic first-person narrator. The dying Hoffmann himself is clearly recognizable in the description of the lamed writer sitting at the window smoking his pipe and wearing cap and dressing gown; and Hoffmann's own experiences may be

assumed behind the creative crisis and melancholy "my
cousin" must overcome. The explanation he gives for having
regained his creative energy forms the theoretical basis of the
ensuing dialogue. "My cousin" withdraws into melancholy by
giving up "the pulsing creative life that emerges from within
me" and renews his desire to live only when life imposes itself
on him from *without*, as viewed from his window. Thus it
seems that there must be two directions to the creative process: the act of imagining, which gives tangible shape to an
inner world, and the act of creative seeing (the German verb
schauen as distinct from *sehen*), which draws on external
reality to give plausibility to the inner visions. Careful observation of the outside world is necessary to provide a solid
foundation for the fantastic elements the imagination may discover beneath the surface of an often banal reality. Thus "my
cousin," who in the past has relied too much on his inner
world, now discovers the inspiration inherent in reality. As he
sits at his window, he then proceeds to instruct the "I," the
initial first-person narrator, in the "first fruits of the art of
seeing," that is, in the pleasure derived from the creative act
of combining accurate observation with imaginative interpre-
tation. With the aid of a telescope, in the course of observing,
describing, and discussing the numerous people who pass
beneath the window the "I" develops a facility for seeing that
rivals, but never matches, his cousin's.

The "I" learns to see in three stages. The first is accurate
observation of details, which he expresses as a listing of
attributes: "—a silk hat . . . a short silk cloak . . . bluish gray
stockings, laced boots . . ." In the second stage he is able to
see more imaginatively so that he recognizes the meaning of
details: "bright scarves and kerchiefs, trinkets calculated to
catch the attention of gullible eyes." The final stage involves
the assembling of random meanings into a coherent charac-

ter; and episodes are even invented to fit the character: "He has a briefcase under his arm—undoubtedly a student on his way to a lecture—." Although the "I" becomes more and more creative and talks more and more fluently, "my cousin" nevertheless remains the dominant figure in the dialogue.

The emphasis on accurate observation in the first part of the narrative does not mean that Hoffmann advocates realism as the only basis of art. Rather, reality must be subjectively transformed into believable possibilities. With his two equally plausible, though in fact totally different characterizations of the tall skinny man with the chest under his arm, "my cousin" demonstrates that subjectivity must be accepted as part of the creative process. Furthermore, his vivid evocation of a nonexistent charcoal burner's family, including a grotesque little humpback, indicates that creative imagination can be altogether independent of observed reality.

At the end of the story "my cousin" reveals the full significance of the act of seeing he has so persuasively advocated: he terms the market "the faithful image of eternally changing life," implying that it represents for him a constant reminder of his own mortality, and yet it continues to renew in him the "courage to live." Thus the creative process itself, inspired by imaginative observation of life, becomes the writer's very means of overcoming death.

The brilliantly entertaining style of *My Cousin's Corner Window* can be appreciated in spite of the story's complex theoretical framework. As in most of his works, Hoffmann ingeniously blends evocative description, amusing aphorisms, learned allusions, ironic deprecation of philistine values, and satirical and grotesque humor into a truly unique verbal texture.

HELENE SCHER

Blond Eckbert

LUDWIG TIECK

IN a region of the Harz there once lived a knight known as
Blond Eckbert. He was about forty years old, of medium
height, and thick, simply cropped light blond hair framed his
pale, gaunt face. He led a quiet, secluded life and was never
involved in the feuds of his neighbors. Rarely was he seen
outside the walls of his small castle. His wife liked solitude as
much as he did, and the two seemed to love each other most
deeply. Their only sorrow was that heaven would not bless
them with children.

Eckbert rarely had guests, and even when visitors did
come, almost nothing in his customary way of life was
changed for their benefit. Moderation reigned in his home,
and frugality seemed to determine all things. On social occasions Eckbert was cheerful and in high spirits, but when he
was alone a certain reserve became apparent in him, a quiet,
restrained melancholy.

No one visited his castle as often as Philip Walther, a man
Eckbert had befriended because he found in him a way of
thinking quite similar to his own. Walther's home was in
Franconia, but he often spent up to half a year at a time near

Eckbert's castle, collecting plants and minerals and sorting
them. Walther possessed a modest fortune and was not
dependent on anyone. Eckbert often joined him on his solitary walks, and every year their friendship grew more intimate.

There are times when man feels anguished that he should
keep a secret from a friend that he may have concealed until
then with great care. The soul has an irresistible urge to confide completely, to disclose its inmost recesses to a friend, so
that he may become an even closer friend. In such moments
gentle souls may reveal themselves completely, and yet it can
happen that the one recoils in fear from knowing the other.

Autumn had arrived when one foggy evening Eckbert sat
with his friend and his wife Bertha by a fire on the hearth.
The flames cast flickering gleams of light into the room and
on the ceiling, black night looked in at the windows, and the
trees outside shivered in the wet cold. Walther complained
about his long trip back home, and Eckbert proposed that he
stay, spend half the night with them in amiable conversation,
and then sleep until morning in one of their rooms. Walther
gladly accepted, and now wine and the evening meal were
brought in, wood was added to the fire, and the friends' conversation became livelier and more intimate.

After the table had been cleared and the servants had left,
Eckbert took Walther's hand and said, "My friend, you really
should have my wife tell you the story of her youth; you'll
see it's quite strange."

"With pleasure," Walther replied, and they gathered
around the hearth again.

It was just midnight, and from time to time the moon
shone through the scudding clouds. "You must not think me
too forward," Bertha began, "but my husband says your
thoughts are so noble that it would be wrong to keep any-

thing from you. Just do not take my story for a fairy tale, no matter how odd it may sound.

"I was born in a little village, my father was a poor shepherd. My parents did not have an easy life, indeed, they often did not know where the next meal would come from. It grieved me far more, however, that my father and mother quarreled about their poverty and often reproached each other bitterly. I was constantly told that I was a stupid, foolish child who could not carry out the simplest tasks; and I really was extremely awkward and clumsy. I was always dropping things, I could not learn how to sew or to spin, I was of no help at all with the housework, but I did understand the misery of my parents very well. Often I would sit in a corner and dream of how I would help them if I suddenly became rich, how I would shower them with gold and silver and would delight in their amazement; I saw spirits emerging that showed me subterranean treasures or gave me pebbles that turned into precious stones; in short, I was lost in the most marvelous daydreams, and whenever I had to get up to help or to carry something, I was even clumsier than before because my head was awhirl with all the strange visions.

"My father was always angry with me because I was such a burden on the household. He often treated me rather cruelly, and I rarely heard him speak a friendly word to me. When I was about eight years old serious efforts were made to get me to do or learn something. My father believed that it was just obstinacy or laziness that made me idle away my days, so he tormented me with threats and admonitions. When that had no effect, he punished me most harshly, adding that this punishment would be repeated every day because I was such a useless creature.

"The whole night I wept bitterly, feeling utterly forlorn and so sorry for myself that I wanted to die. I feared daybreak, I really did not know what I should do, I wished I had all kinds of skills and just could not understand why I was more backward than the other children I knew. I was near despair.

"I got up when day began to dawn and, almost without knowing it, I unlatched the door of our little hut. I found myself in the open fields, and soon afterward I was in a forest hardly penetrated by the light of day. I ran without looking back and without feeling tired, for I was afraid my father would catch up with me and, provoked by my running away, would treat me even more cruelly.

"When I emerged from the forest the sun was already quite high, and in front of me I saw a strange darkness covered with fog. Soon I had to climb over hills, then I had to follow a path winding between huge boulders, and, realizing I must be in the neighboring mountains, I became frightened in my solitude. Down in the plain I had never seen any mountains, and the very word mountain itself, whenever I had heard it mentioned, had had a horrible sound to my innocent ear. But I did not have the heart to go back; my fear drove me on. I often looked around in alarm when the wind passed through the trees over me or the sound of a woodcutter's axe echoed through the still morning. When I finally met some miners and charcoal burners and heard an unfamiliar accent, I almost fainted in terror.

"I came through several villages and began to beg, for I was hungry and thirsty. When questioned, I managed to get by on my answers. I had been wandering in this way for about four days when I found myself on a narrow path that took me farther and farther away from the main road. The rocks around me now had a different, much stranger appearance. There were boulders piled so high that it looked as if the first gust of wind would topple them in confusion. I did not know whether I should go on. As it was the best season of the year, at night I always slept in the forest or in remote shepherd huts; here, however, I did not see a single human dwelling and could not expect to find one in this wilderness. The cliffs and crags got more and more terrifying, often I had to pass close by to a dizzying precipice, and finally the path ended beneath my feet. I was completely desolate, I cried and screamed, and my voice echoed back to me from the rocky valleys with a horrifying sound. Now night fell, and I looked for a mossy spot to rest on. I could not sleep. During the night I heard the strangest sounds; sometimes I thought it was wild animals, sometimes the wind moaning through the rocks, sometimes weird birds. I prayed, and only toward morning did I fall asleep.

"I woke up when daylight shone on my face. In front of me was a steep boulder; I scrambled up it in the hope of being able to discover a way out of the wilderness and perhaps houses or people. But when I was on top, everything as far as my eye could see was just like right around me, everything was covered with a veil of fog, the day was gray and gloomy, and I could not see a single tree or meadow, not even a bush except for a few stunted and solitary shrubs growing out of clefts in the rock. I cannot describe the longing I felt to catch sight of another human being, even if I would have to be afraid of him. Tortured too by ravenous pangs of hunger, I sat down and decided to die. But in a while the desire to live won out after all. I gathered up all my strength and walked on for the entire day amidst tears and sobs. In the end I hardly knew what I was doing, I was tired and exhausted, I scarcely wished to live and yet I feared death.

"Toward evening the landscape seemed to be getting somewhat less hostile, my thoughts and wishes came alive once more, the desire for life surged anew in all my veins. I thought I heard the murmur of a millwheel in the distance, so I walked faster, and how glad, how relieved I felt when at last I actually did reach the end of the rocky wilderness and saw woods and meadows again with distant, pleasant hills! It seemed to me as if I had stepped out of hell into a paradise; my solitude and helplessness no longer frightened me.

"Instead of the mill I had hoped to find, I came upon a waterfall, so my spirits sank somewhat. I was scooping up some water from the brook to drink when suddenly I thought I heard a soft cough at some distance. Never have I been so pleasantly surprised as at that moment! I went closer and discovered an old woman sitting at the edge of the forest who appeared to be resting. She was dressed almost completely in black, a black bonnet covered her head and much of her face, and in her hand she held a crutch.

"I approached her and asked her for help. She let me sit down next to her and gave me some bread and wine. While I was eating, she sang a hymn in a shrill voice. When she had finished, she said I should follow her.

"I was glad to accept the old woman's offer, no matter how queer her voice and manner seemed. With her crutch she walked quite nimbly, making such a grimace at every step that at first I had to laugh. The wild mountains receded farther and farther behind us; we went across a pleasant meadow and then through a sizable forest. When we emerged from it, the sun was just setting, and I will never forget the sight and sensations of that evening. Everything was dissolved in the softest red and gold, the trees stood with their tops glowing in the sunset, and over the fields lay an enchanting light; the woods and the leaves of the trees stood motionless, the clear heavens looked like an opened paradise, and the murmur of the brooks and the occasional whispering of the

trees sounded through the serene stillness as if in melancholy
joy. For the first time my young soul sensed the meaning of
the world and its affairs. I forget myself and my guide; my
spirit and my eyes hovered enraptured amidst the golden
clouds.

"We now climbed up a hill covered with birch trees. From
the top I could see a green valley full of birches, and among
the trees below was a little hut. I could hear lively barking,
and soon a nimble little dog jumped up at the old woman,
wagging its tail; then it came up to me, sniffed at me from all
sides, and with friendly gestures returned to the old woman.

"As we came down the hill I heard a marvelous song that
seemed to be coming from the hut, as if from a bird. This was
sung:

> Alone in the wood,
> I feel oh, so good,
> Tomorrow, today,
> For ever and aye.
> Oh, I'm so gay,
> In the wood I'll stay.

"These few words were repeated again and again. Were I
to describe the sound, it was almost as if far away hunting
horns and reeded shawm joined in harmony.

"My curiosity knew no bounds. Without waiting for word
from the old woman, I entered the hut. It was twilight; everything looked very tidy; some bowls were lined up on a cup-
board, odd-looking jars stood on a table, in a shiny cage
hanging at the window there was a bird, and it really was this
bird that sang the words. The old woman coughed and
gasped, she seemed not to be able to recover from her exer-
tions; she alternately patted the little dog and talked with the

bird, which answered only with its usual song; as for me, she acted as if I were not there. While I was watching her, chills ran up and down my spine, for her face was in constant motion; moreover, her head shook as if from old age so that I could not tell at all what she really looked like.

"When she had recovered she lit the lamp, set a small table and brought out supper. Now she looked around for me and told me to sit down in one of the wicker chairs. So I sat facing her, and the lamp stood between us. She folded her bony hands and prayed aloud, continuing her facial contortions so that I almost had to laugh again, but I controlled myself so as not to make her angry.

"After supper she prayed again and then showed me to a bed in a tiny alcove. She herself slept in the main room. Since I was half dazed, I did not stay awake long, but during the night I woke up a few times and heard the old woman coughing and speaking with her dog, and, at intervals, I heard the bird, which seemed to be dreaming and was singing just single words of its song. Together with the birch trees rustling outside the window and the sound of a distant nightingale, this made such a wondrous mixture that I never felt I had awakened, but rather as if I were falling into another, still stranger dream.

"In the morning the old woman woke me up and directed me to my work. I had to spin, which now I easily learned, and I also had to take care of the dog and the bird. I quickly got used to running the household. Soon I felt as if everything had to be the way it was. I no longer thought that there was something strange about the old woman, that her dwelling was odd and far away from all human beings, and that there was something extraordinary about the bird. Yet I was struck again and again by its beauty, for its feathers shone with myriad colors, the most beautiful light blue and a fiery red alternated on its neck and body, and whenever it sang it puffed itself up in pride so that its feathers were displayed even more magnificently.

"The old woman often went away and did not return until evening. On those occasions I would go out with the dog to meet her, and she would call me her child and daughter. In the end I became very attached to her, as our mind will get used to everything, especially in childhood. In the evening hours she taught me how to read. I learned easily, and reading later became a source of boundless pleasure for me in my solitude, for she had some old books that contained the most marvelous stories.

"The memory of my life at that time seems strange to me even now. No one ever visited me, yet I felt secure and at home in the cozy little family, for the dog and the bird fostered an affection in me that only longtime friends are known to share. I have never been able to recall the dog's strange name, though I said it so often.

"I had been living with the old woman for four years and was about twelve years old when she began to trust me more and finally told me a secret: Every day the bird laid an egg which contained a pearl or some other precious stone. I had noticed that the old woman secretively puttered around the cage, but I had never paid closer heed. Now she gave me the task of collecting these eggs in her absence and storing them in the odd-looking jars. She left food for me and would now stay away longer, sometimes for weeks or months; my spinning wheel hummed, the dog barked, the marvelous bird sang, while all around me there was such calm that I cannot remember a single storm the whole time I was there. No one happened upon me by chance, no wild animals came near our dwelling, I was content and worked the days away. Man would perhaps be quite happy if he could live his life out in such undisturbed tranquillity.

"From the little I read I developed rather peculiar ideas about the world and mankind, for I based everything on myself and my companions. When I read about happy people I could not imagine they were any different from the little dog; splendid ladies always looked like the bird, all old women like my own weird mistress. I had also read something about love, and in my imagination I acted out strange stories. I envisioned the handsomest knight in the world, I decked him out with every imaginable excellence, without really knowing what he looked like after all my efforts, but I could feel very sorry for myself if he did not return my love; then I recited long sentimental speeches to myself, sometimes aloud, in order to win him over. You are smiling! All of us, of course, are long since past this stage of youth.

"Now I preferred to be alone, for then I was the sole mistress of the house. The dog loved me and did everything I wanted, the bird responded to all my questions with its song, my spinning wheel turned merrily, and so I never felt any desire for change. When the old woman returned from her long wanderings, she praised my attentiveness, saying that since I was there her household was much tidier, she was pleased with my growth and my healthy appearance; in short, she treated me completely like a daughter.

" 'You are very good, my child!' she once said to me in rasping tones, 'if you continue like this, things will always go well for you: but no good will come of straying from the right path, punishment will follow, sooner or later.' Since I was quite a lively and impulsive child, I did not pay much attention to what she said, but during the night it occurred to me again and I could not understand what she had meant. I carefully pondered every word. I had read about great riches, and at last it occurred to me that her pearls and precious stones might be very valuable. Slowly I understood more and more. But what did the right path mean? I just could not explain.

"It is man's misfortune that he gains understanding only to lose the innocence of his soul. I was now fourteen years old and well aware that it was only up to me to take the bird and the precious stones in the old woman's absence and go out into the world I had read so much about. Then perhaps I would meet the glorious knight of my dreams.

"At first, this was just like any other thought, but as I sat at my spinning wheel it occurred to me again. Soon I was so engrossed that I saw myself gloriously attired, surrounded by knights and princes. I could get very sad when I looked up from such dreams and found myself in the little hut again. Yet, if I did my tasks the old woman did not seem concerned.

"One day my mistress left again, saying that this time she would stay away longer than usual: I should take good care of everything and not let the time drag by too slowly. I said goodbye to her with a certain sense of foreboding, for I felt I was never to see her again. My eyes followed her for a long time. I did not know why I was so frightened; it was almost as if, without my fully realizing it, my plans were already made.

"Never before did I take care of the dog and the bird so attentively; I was more attached to them than ever. The old woman had already been gone for a few days when I got up one morning firmly resolved to leave the hut, take the bird with me, and see what the world was like. I felt constricted and oppressed. First I wanted to stay after all and then I couldn't bear the thought. There was a strange conflict in my soul as if two rebellious spirits were struggling within me. At one moment the peaceful solitude seemed so beautiful to me, at the next I was enraptured again with the image of a new world in all its marvelous diversity.

"I did not know what to make of myself; the dog kept jumping up at me, bright sunshine spread over the fields, the green birch trees glistened. I had the feeling that I was in a great hurry, so I grabbed the little dog, tied it up in the room, and took the cage with the bird under my arm. The dog wriggled and whined at this unaccustomed treatment, it looked at me with pleading eyes, but I was afraid to take it along. I did take one of the jars filled with precious stones, but I left all the rest.

"The bird turned its head in a peculiar way when I carried it out the door; the dog struggled hard to follow me but had to stay behind.

"I avoided the path toward the rocky wilderness and went in the opposite direction. The dog continued to bark and whimper, and I was touched to the heart. Several times the bird tried to sing but seemed too uncomfortable to do so while being carried.

"The farther I went, the less I heard the barking, and finally it ceased altogether. I wept and almost turned back, but the desire to see something new drove me on.

"I had already gone over the hills and through some woods when evening came and I sought shelter in a village. I was very timid when I entered the inn. I was shown a room and a bed and slept quite peacefully, except that I dreamed of the old woman and she was threatening me.

"My trip did not have much variety, but the farther I went, the more I was alarmed by the thought of the old woman and the little dog. I believed that without my help the dog would starve, and in the forest I often imagined that the old woman would suddenly stand in my way. With many sighs and tears I traveled on. Every time I rested and put the cage on the ground, the bird sang its marvelous song and I vividly recalled the beautiful spot I had left. As human nature is forgetful, I now thought that the earlier trip in my childhood was not as wretched as the present one, and I wished I could be back in that situation again.

"I had sold some precious stones and, after wandering for many days, I arrived in a village. The minute I entered it I had a strange feeling; I was frightened but did not know why. Soon I realized that it was the very village in which I was born. How surprised I was! How the tears ran down my cheeks with joy, with a thousand strange memories! A great deal had changed; new houses had been built, others that had been new had fallen into disrepair, fires had also left their traces. Everything was much smaller and more cramped than I had expected. Joyously I looked forward to seeing my parents again after so many years. I found the little house, the well-known threshold; the doorlatch was still as it always had been, it seemed to me that I had shut the door only yesterday. My heart pounded violently as I hastily opened the door—but inside there were completely unknown faces staring at me in astonishment. I asked for Martin the shepherd and was told that he and his wife had died three years before. I quickly withdrew and left the village sobbing loudly.

"I had imagined how nice it would be to surprise my parents with my riches; through a strange coincidence, what I had only dreamed of in childhood had come true—and now everything was in vain, they could no longer rejoice with me, and what I had most hoped for in life was lost to me forever.

"In a pleasant town I rented a small house with a garden and found myself a maid. The world did not seem to be as marvelous as I had imagined, but I began to forget the old woman and my stay with her, and on the whole I lived quite contentedly.

"The bird had not sung for a long time. I was therefore quite alarmed when one night it suddenly started to sing again, but with different words. It sang:

> Alone in the wood,
> I'd go back if I could.
> You're sure to pay
> Some later day.
> Oh, I'd be gay
> In the wood far away.

"I could not sleep the entire night; all my memories came alive again, and more than ever I felt that I had done wrong. When I got up I could not bear the sight of the bird; it kept looking at me, and its presence frightened me. It would not stop repeating its song and sang louder and more forcefully than ever before. The more I looked at it, the more alarmed I became. Finally I opened the cage, stuck my hand in, grasped its neck, and firmly pressed my fingers together; it looked at me pleadingly, I let go, but it had already died. I buried it in the garden.

"Now I often felt afraid of my maid. Looking back on my past, I imagined that she too could steal some day or even kill me.

"For quite some time I had known a young knight whom I liked very much. I gave him my hand in marriage—and with this, Mr. Walther, my story is at an end."

"You should have seen her then," Eckbert hastily interrupted, "seen her youth, her beauty, and the inconceivable charm that her secluded upbringing had given her. She seemed to be a miracle, and my love knew no bounds. I had no fortune, yet she brought me prosperity; we moved here, and we have not regretted our union for a moment."

"But while we have been talking," Bertha replied, "it has become very late—let us go to sleep."

She stood up to leave. Kissing her hand, Walther wished her good night and said, "Dear lady, I thank you. I can really well imagine you with the strange bird and how you fed little *Strohmian*."

Walther too went to bed. Only Eckbert still paced restlessly up and down the room. "Is man not a fool?" he said at last. "I myself made my wife tell her story, and now I regret this confidence! Won't he abuse it? Won't he tell it to others? Won't he perhaps—for such is human nature—be seized by greed for our precious stones and then, still pretending to be our friend, conspire to steal them?"

It occurred to him that Walther had not said good night with the sincerity he would have thought natural after such intimacy. Once the soul is aroused to suspicion, it finds confirmation in every trifle. Eckbert reproached himself for his base mistrust of his good friend, yet he could not free himself from it. The whole night he struggled with these thoughts and slept very little.

The next morning Bertha was ill and could not come to breakfast. Walther did not seem to be much concerned and took leave of the knight with an air of indifference. Eckbert could not understand his behavior. He went to see his wife and found her with a high fever. She said that last night's story must have strained her unduly.

From that night on Walther visited the castle of his friend only rarely, and when he did come he left again after a few noncommittal words. Eckbert was much tormented by this behavior. Although he concealed his feelings from Bertha and Walther, anyone could notice his inner agitation.

To the doctor's alarm, Bertha's illness became critical. The color left her cheeks, and her eyes burned with fever. One

morning she called her husband to her bedside and sent out
the servants.

"Dear husband," she began, "I must disclose something to
you that has almost driven me out of my mind, that is ruining
my health though it may seem to be a mere trifle.

"You know that whenever I spoke of my childhood, no
matter how hard I tried I could never remember the name of
the little dog I spent so much time with. But on the night of
my story, Walther suddenly said to me when retiring, 'I can
well imagine how you fed little *Strohmian.*' Is that a coincidence? Did he guess the name, did he know it and mention it
deliberately? And what does this man have to do with my
fate? Sometimes I struggle with myself as if I were only imagining this mystery, but it is certain, all too certain. I was
seized with terror when a stranger could help me to find my
memories. What do you think, Eckbert?"

Eckbert looked at his suffering wife with deep compassion.
Lost in silent reflection for a while, he then said a few comforting words and left her. In a remote room of his castle he
paced up and down in indescribable agitation. For many
years Walther had been his sole companion, and yet now he
was the only person in the world whose existence oppressed
and tormented him. It seemed as though he would feel happy
and relieved if only this one person could be gotten out of the
way. In order to distract himself, he took down his crossbow
and went hunting.

It was a raw, stormy winter day; deep snow lay on the
mountains and bent down the branches of the trees. He
roamed about, sweat stood on his brow; he found no game,
and this made his mood even worse. Suddenly he saw something move in the distance: it was Walther collecting moss
from the trees. Without knowing what he was doing, Eckbert
took out an arrow, aimed, Walther looked around, made a

threatening gesture, but the arrow flew from the bow, and Walther fell to the ground.

Eckbert felt relieved and reassured, but a shudder drove him back to his castle. He had a long way to go, for he had strayed deep into the forest. When he arrived, Bertha had already died. Before her death she had spoken at length of Walther and the old woman.

Eckbert lived for a long time in total solitude. He had always been melancholy by nature because his wife's strange story had troubled him all along and he had feared that something unfortunate might occur, but now he was completely at odds with himself. He was haunted by the murder of his friend, ravaged by deepest remorse.

In order to distract himself, he sometimes went to the nearest city where he attended various social gatherings. He longed for a friend to fill the void in his soul, but whenever he remembered Walther he was frightened at the very thought of finding a friend. He was convinced that no friend could ever make him happy. He had lived with Bertha for such a long time in peace, Walther's friendship had made him happy for so many years, and now both of them had so suddenly been taken from him that at certain moments his life seemed more like a strange fairy tale than an actual existence.

A young knight named Hugo sought contact with the quiet and melancholy Eckbert, appearing to have a definite affection for him. With a wonderful feeling of surprise, Eckbert returned the knight's friendship, all the more willingly since he had never expected it. Now the two were often together, Hugo showed Eckbert every possible kindness; the one almost never rode out without the other, they appeared together on all social occasions; in short, they seemed inseparable.

Eckbert could not be happy for more than brief moments,

believing that Hugo liked him only by mistake. Hugo did not know him, did not know his story. Again he felt the urge to confide completely so that he could be sure that Hugo was truly his friend, yet doubts and the fear of being detested held him back. Sometimes Eckbert was so convinced of his baseness that he thought only a total stranger could ever respect him. Nevertheless he could not resist the urge, and during a solitary horseback ride he revealed his entire story to his friend, asking him whether he could like a murderer. Hugo was touched and tried to comfort him. Relieved, Eckbert returned with his companion to the city in better spirits.

It seemed, however, that he was cursed with becoming suspicious exactly at the moment of greatest trust, for they had hardly entered the hall when in the glow of the many lights the facial expressions of his friend began to displease him. He thought he noticed a malicious smile; he was struck by the fact that Hugo rarely spoke with him, but all the more with others, and, indeed, scarcely seemed to pay any attention to him. Among the guests there was an old knight who had always been Eckbert's enemy and had often inquired in a singular way about his wealth and his wife. Hugo now joined the old man, and the two spoke secretively at length, often pointing to Eckbert. Confirmed in his suspicions, Eckbert thought himself betrayed, and a horrible rage overcame him. With his eyes fixed on them, he suddenly saw Walther's face, all of his expressions and gestures, the whole figure so well known to him. He continued to stare and became convinced that no one else but Walther was speaking with the old man. Eckbert's terror was indescribable; beside himself he dashed out of the hall, left the city that very night, and found his way back to his castle only after wandering about for a long time.

Like a restless spirit he rushed from room to room, unable to focus his thoughts. He sank from terrifying visions to still more terrifying ones and could find no sleep. Often he thought he was insane and only created everything in his imagination; then he recalled Walther's features, and everything became more and more of a mystery. He decided to take a trip so that he might bring some order to his thoughts. By now he had given up forever the thought of friendship, the desire for companionship.

He set out without a clear destination; indeed, he scarcely noticed his surroundings. When he had been pushing his horse at the fastest gallop for several days, he suddenly saw he had strayed into a labyrinth of rocks with no way out. At last he met a peasant who showed him a path along a waterfall. In gratitude Eckbert offered him a few coins, but the peasant would not accept them. "Let's see," Eckbert said to himself, "whether I can imagine that he too was no one else but Walther." And when he looked up again, it was indeed no one else but Walther. Eckbert spurred his horse on as fast as it could gallop, through meadows and forests, until the animal dropped beneath him from exhaustion. Unconcerned, he continued his trip on foot.

As if in a dream he climbed up a hill. He thought he could hear lively barking nearby, birch trees rustled, and then he heard a song in strange tones:

> Once more in the wood,
> I feel oh, so good.
> Grief's far away,
> No envy does prey.
> Again I'm so gay,
> In the wood I'll stay.

Now Eckbert was done for, his consciousness, his senses left him. He could not find his way out of the mystery whether he was dreaming now or had been dreaming of a wife named Bertha. The most marvelous things mingled with the most ordinary, the world around him was enchanted, and he was incapable of a single thought, a single memory.

An old woman bent with age crept up the hill on a crutch, coughing. "Are you bringing me my bird? My pearls? My dog?" she shrieked at him. "You see, injustice punishes itself: no one else but I was your friend Walther, your Hugo."

"God in heaven!" Eckbert mumbled to himself. "In what dreadful solitude have I spent my life!"

"And Bertha was your sister."

Eckbert sank to the ground.

"Why did she leave me deceitfully? Otherwise everything would have turned out well, for her trial period was already over. She was the daughter of a knight, who had her brought up by a shepherd, your father's daughter."

"Why have I always suspected this horrible thought?" Eckbert cried out.

"Because in your childhood you once heard your father talk about it. His wife would not allow him to bring up his daughter himself, as she was the child of another woman."

Eckbert lay on the ground, insane and dying. Numbed and bewildered, he heard the old woman speaking, the dog barking, and the bird repeating its song.

The Story of Honest Casper and Fair Annie

CLEMENS BRENTANO

IT was early summer. The nightingales had only just begun to sing, but they were silent on that cool night with a chill wind from distant storms in the air. The night watchman was calling out the eleventh hour when, on my way home, I saw a group of young men, just come from the tavern, clustered around someone sitting on the doorstep of a large building. They seemed so distressed that I went up to them, fearing that some accident had occurred.

An old peasant woman was sitting there on the steps. However solicitous the bystanders' concern was, she appeared oblivious to their curiosity and well-meant suggestions. There was something uncanny, even majestic, about the way the dear old woman knew exactly what she wanted to do. In the midst of all those people she made herself comfortable for a night out in the open as calmly as if she were alone in her own bedroom. She drew her apron around her as a cover, pulled her big black oilcloth hat down over her eyes, patted her traveling bundle into a pillow under her head, and would not react to a single question.

21

"What's wrong with the old woman?" I asked one of the bystanders.

Answers came from all sides: "She has walked in twenty miles from the country; she's exhausted; she's lost here in the city; she has friends at the other end of town but can't find the way."

"I wanted to take her there," someone said, "but it's quite far and I've forgotten my house key. Besides, she would not recognize the house she's looking for."

"But the woman just can't stay here over night," remarked a newcomer.

"She insists on staying," replied the first. "I've told her I'd take her home, but her answers don't make sense. Perhaps she's drunk."

"I think she's crazy. But she just can't stay here," the other repeated, "the night is long and cool."

During all of this talk the old woman had finished making herself comfortable, as little disturbed as if she were deaf and blind. When someone repeated: "But she just can't stay here," she answered in a strangely deep and serious voice:

"Why can't I stay here, isn't this the duke's house? I am eighty-eight years old, and surely the duke won't drive me away from his doorstep. My three sons died in his service, and my only grandson has departed. I'm sure God will forgive him, and I refuse to die until he gets an honorable burial."

"Eighty-eight years old and a twenty-mile walk!" exclaimed the bystanders. "She's tired and childish; one becomes frail at such an advanced age."

"Mother, you'll catch cold here and get sick, and you'll be lonely too," someone said and bent down toward her.

Then the old woman spoke again in her deep voice, half pleading, half commanding:

"Oh leave me in peace and be sensible! I've no use for a cold, and I'm not going to be lonely. It's already late, I'm eighty-eight years old, morning will soon be here, and then I'll go to my friends. If a person is pious, trusts fate, and can pray, he'll be able to get through a few short hours."

The bystanders gradually dispersed, and when the night watchman appeared again, the last ones rushed away to have him unlock their house doors for them. I was the only one left. The streets became very still. Lost in reflection, I walked back and forth under the trees of the open square. I had been deeply affected by the old woman's manner, her serious, determined tone, her self-assurance after eighty-eight years of changing seasons, a long life that she seemed to regard as but the portal to a blessed sanctuary. "What are all the sufferings, all the desires of my heart? With eternal indifference the stars continue on their way. To what purpose do I seek refreshment and comfort, and from whom do I seek them and for whom? Whatever I seek and love and gain, will it ever make me able to spend the night on the doorstep, awaiting morning, with as much composure as this dear pious soul? And will I then find my friend, as she surely will? Oh, I'll never even reach the city, I'll collapse from exhaustion in the dust before the city gate and perhaps fall into the hands of robbers." Such were my thoughts. As I walked under the linden trees and approached the old woman again, I heard her praying aloud with head bowed. I was strangely affected and went up to her, saying: "In God's name, good mother, include me in your prayers!" Then I slipped a silver thaler into her apron.

With complete composure the old woman replied: "A thousand thanks, Master, that you have answered my prayer."

I thought she was speaking to me and said: "Mother, did you ask me for something? I was not aware of it."

Startled, the old woman turned to me and said: "Dear sir, do go home, say your prayers, and lie down to sleep. What are you doing out on the streets so late at night? That's not at all good for young fellows; the enemy lurks and waits that he may come upon you. Many a person has come to grief by roaming about at such a late hour. Whom do you seek? The Lord? He may be found in the hearts of men, if they be righteous, and not on the streets. But if you seek the enemy, you've found him already. Go home now and pray that you may be rid of him. Good night."

With these words she quietly turned away, putting the coin into her bundle. Everything the old woman did made a strange and serious impression on me, so I spoke again:

"Good mother, you're undoubtedly right, but it's because of you I'm still here. I heard your prayers and wanted to beg you to include me in them."

"I've already done that," she said. "When I noticed you walking back and forth under the linden trees, I prayed that God grant you good thoughts. Now you have them, go home and sleep well."

Instead, I sat down on the steps next to her, grasped her wrinkled hand and said: "Let me sit here beside you through the night, while you tell me where you're from and why you are here in the city. You'll not get any help here; at your age one is closer to God than to man. The world has changed since you were young."

"I know," the old woman replied, "yet throughout my life I've found the world much the same. You are still young; at your age one can still be surprised. But I have seen so much of life repeat itself that now I look upon all of it only with pleasure, because God is so faithful. But one should never turn good will away, even if it's not needed, lest the good friend fail to appear at another time when he'd be most welcome. So stay where you are, and let's see if you can help me.

I'll tell you what has made me walk so many miles to the city.
I never thought I would ever come here again. Seventy years
ago I worked as a maid in the very house where I now sit on
the doorstep. Since then I've not been to the city again. How
time flies, like the turning of a hand. How often I sat here in
the evening seventy years ago and waited for my sweetheart,
who served as a soldier in the regiment. It was here that we
pledged our love. When he—but hush, here comes the guard
patrol."

There on the doorstep she then started to sing in hushed
tones, as young maids and servants do on beautiful moonlit
nights. With great pleasure I heard her sing this old sweet
song:

> When Judgment Day shall come to be,
> The stars shall fall on land and sea.
> Ye dead, ye dead shall all be raised,
> At Judgment's seat to be appraised;
> On tiptoe ye shall humbly go
> Where the blessed angels sit in row.
> Our dear God waits there, newly come
> With a glorious rainbow 'round him spun.
> Trembling those false Jews there must stand
> Who gave our Lord to Pilate's hand.
> The tallest trees shed radiance near,
> The hardest stones are crushed with fear.
> If you this short sweet prayer can say
> And surely pray it once a day,
> The soul will then face God with cheer,
> When at Heaven's gates we do appear!
> Amen.

As the patrol approached us, the old woman exclaimed
with emotion: "Oh, today is the sixteenth of May; every-

thing's the same, just as it was then, only they're wearing different caps and no longer have pigtails. No matter, if they're good at heart!" The officer of the guard stopped and was about to ask what we were doing here so late when I recognized him as an acquaintance of mine, Corporal Count Grossinger. I briefly described the situation to him, whereupon he said, deeply moved: "Take this thaler for the old woman and a rose too"—he held one in his hand—"old peasants are fond of flowers. Tomorrow please ask the old woman to repeat the song to you, so you can write it down for me. For a long time I've been trying to find that song and have never come across the complete version."

Then we parted, for as we approached guard headquarters across the square, the sentry called out: "Who's there?"

As Grossinger left, he told me he had guard duty at the castle and I should visit him there. I returned to the old woman and gave her the rose and the thaler.

In an outburst of emotion she seized the rose and fastened it to her hat, murmuring in a gentle, quavering voice:

> "Roses the flowers on the hat I wear,
> If I were rich I'd have no care,
> Roses and my sweetheart."

I exclaimed: "Goodness, mother, you've become quite gay!" and she recited:

> Gay, so gay,
> Away and away,
> Night and day,
> Here he'd stay,
> Now gone his way,
> Wonder you may!

"You see, dear sir, isn't it good I stayed out here? Everything's the same, believe me. It was seventy years ago to the day that I sat here on the doorstep. I was a sprightly young maid, fond of singing all the old songs. Just like today, I was singing the Judgment Day song when the patrol went by, and a passing grenadier threw a rose into my lap—I still have the petals in my Bible—and that's when I first met my dear husband. The next morning I wore the rose to church; he recognized me and we got to know each other. That's why I'm so pleased to get a rose again today. It's a sign that I should come to him! How I rejoice! Four sons and a daughter have been taken from me, the day before yesterday my grandson left me—may God help him and have mercy on him!—and tomorrow another good soul will leave me. But why do I say tomorrow? Is it not already past midnight?"

"Yes, the hour of twelve has struck," I answered, astonished at her words.

"May God grant her peace and comfort for the four short hours left to her!" said the old woman and fell silent, folding her hands as in prayer. Her words and whole manner affected me so intensely that I too could not speak. But her silence endured, and since the coin from the officer was still in her lap, I said: "Mother, put the thaler away or you'll lose it."

"I won't put it away, I'll give it to my friend in her last hour of distress!" she replied. "The first thaler I'll take home with me tomorrow, my grandson shall have it. You see, he was a fine boy, always so scrupulous about his person and about his soul—O God, about his soul!—I prayed the whole way here; the dear Lord will surely have mercy on him. Of all the boys in school he was always the cleanest and most hard-working, but the most astonishing thing about him was his sense of honor. His lieutenant often said: 'If my company has a sense of honor, it comes from Casper Finkel's quarters.'

He was in the cavalry. When he first returned from France he had many fine stories to tell, but they all had something to do with honor. His father and stepbrother served in the militia. There often were arguments about honor, for while he had it in excess, they did not have enough. God forgive me my great sin, I do not mean to speak ill of them. Everyone has his own burden to bear; but my poor dead daughter, *his* mother, worked herself to death for that lazy good-for-nothing, she just could not pay off his debts.

"Well, Cavalryman Casper talked a lot about the Frenchmen, but when his father and stepbrother did not have a single good word to say about them, he said: 'Father, you don't understand, they have a great sense of honor.' His stepbrother replied maliciously: 'How can you talk so glibly about honor to your father? After all, he was an officer in the N . . . Regiment and really ought to know more about it than you, a mere private.' 'Yes,' old Finkel said with growing annoyance, 'I indeed was an officer and gave many an arrogant young fellow his twenty-five blows; if I'd had some Frenchmen in the company, they'd have felt them even more, with their sense of honor!' These words caused the cavalryman much grief, and he said: 'I have a story about a French petty officer that I like better. During the reign of the former king there was much talk about introducing corporal punishment for discipline in the French army. At a big parade in Strasbourg an order of the War Minister was proclaimed, and the troops in rank and file listened to the proclamation in grim silence. At the end of the parade, a private was ruled out of order, and his petty officer was commanded to give him twelve blows. It was a strict command, so the officer had no choice but to obey. When he was through, he took the rifle of the private he had just beaten, stuck it into the ground in front of himself and released the trigger with his foot so that a bullet went through his head, and the officer sank down dead. When the king heard of the incident, he immediately ordered that corporal punishment should be discontinued. You see, father, that fellow had a true sense of honor!' 'He was a fool,' exclaimed the stepbrother. 'Eat your honor, if you're hungry!' grumbled the father.

"Then my grandson took his sword, left the house, came straight to me and, amidst bitter tears, told me everything. I could not console him; although I could not entirely discredit the story he told me, I always said in the end: 'To God alone be honor!' I gave him my blessing, as his furlough was over the next day and he still wanted to ride a few miles to the town where my goddaughter was a servant on an estate. He was so attached to this girl that he thought he would share his life with her—and they'll soon be united, if God hears my prayers. He has already departed, my goddaughter will go today. I've prepared the dowry. No one will be present at the wedding but me."

The old woman fell silent again and seemed to be praying. All kinds of thoughts about honor kept running through my mind. Was it right for a Christian to accept the death of the petty officer as noble and proper? I wish someone could give me a convincing answer.

When the night watchman called out one o'clock, the old woman sighed: "I have two hours left! Oh my, you're still here. Why don't you go home to bed. You won't be able to work tomorrow, and your master will scold you. What's your trade, dear sir?"

I had no idea how I could explain to her that I was a writer. If I said I was a scholar, I'd be lying. How strange that a German always feels a bit ashamed to say he's a writer (*Schriftsteller*); and he is especially reluctant to use the word in speaking with the lower classes, as they would all too readily think of the scribes and Pharisees from the Bible. The word *Schriftsteller* has not been as generally accepted among the Germans as the term *homme de lettres* among the French. The French are truly skilled writers, and in their works they tend to rely more on an established professional tradition. Indeed, the question is often asked: *"Où avez-vous fait votre philosophie*, where were you trained in philosophy?"*; and in general the French have more of the "man of training" in them. But it's not only this un-German custom that makes it embarrassing to say writer when you're asked at the city gate to state who you are. A certain inner shame makes us reticent, a feeling that comes over everyone who does business with free spiritual goods, with heaven-sent gifts. Scholars can afford to be less embarrassed than poets, for they usually have paid for their training and often serve the state by cracking hard nuts or by working deep in the earth where wild streams are to be pumped out and tamed. But the poet, so-called, is worst off, since more often than not he ran straight from the schoolyard to climb Parnassus; and suspicion must indeed fall on someone who has no other profession than that of a poet. How easy it is to reproach him: "My dear sir, every person alive has poetry in him, just as he has a brain, heart, stomach, spleen, liver, and the like. But someone who concentrates too much on one of these organs, feeds it too much, and develops it to the exclusion of all others, even going to the extreme of making it a means of livelihood, that person ought to feel terribly ashamed when confronted with his fellow men. Someone who lives by poetry alone has lost all balance; an enlarged goose liver, after all, no matter how good it tastes, does come from a sick goose." Anyone who does not earn his bread by the sweat of his brow must feel some sense of shame, particularly someone who is forced to call himself a writer before he has had some success. Such

thoughts went through my mind as I pondered my reply to
the old woman. She was astonished at my hesitancy and said:

"What's your trade, I ask. Why won't you tell me? If it's
not an honest trade, then learn a new one; an honest trade is
its own reward. You're not by chance a hangman or a spy
out to get me, are you? It's all the same, whatever you are,
just tell me! If I saw you sitting around idly during the day,
I'd think you were a do-nothing or sluggard who must lean
against house walls so he won't fall over from sheer laziness."

A word finally occurred to me that might bridge the gap
between us. "Good mother," I said, "I am a clerk."

"Well," she said, "you could have told me that sooner. So
you're a man of the pen. You'll need a good mind for that,
quick fingers and a good heart, otherwise you won't get far.
So you're a clerk? In that case, perhaps you could write a
petition to the duke for me. But it must be one that will
surely be read and won't get buried among all the others."

"Of course I can write a petition for you, mother," I said,
"and I'll try hard to make it as convincing as possible."

"Well, that's nice of you," she replied. "May God reward
you for it. May you live longer than I have, and in your old
age may He grant you, as He did me, calm and composure
and a beautiful night with roses and thalers, and a friend, too,
who will set up a petition for you if you need it. But go home
now, dear sir, fetch a piece of paper and write the petition.
I'll wait here for you one more hour and then I'll go to my
goddaughter. You can come along, she'll be pleased with the
petition. She has a good heart, but God's judgments are wondrous."

After these words the old woman again fell silent, bowed
her head, and seemed to be praying. The thaler still lay in her
lap. When she started to cry, I said: "Good mother, what's
wrong? From what sadness come these tears?"

"Well, why shouldn't I cry? I'm crying about the thaler, about the petition, about everything. But what's the use, everything here on earth is much, much better than we humans deserve, and the bitterest tears are still much too sweet. Just look at the golden camel over there on the apothecary's sign. Marvelous and glorious are God's creations, but man does not understand. It is easier for such a camel to go through the eye of a needle, than for a rich man to enter into the kingdom of God. But why are you still sitting there? Go fetch some paper and bring me the petition."

"Good mother," I replied, "how can I set up a petition for you if you don't tell me what I should say in it?"

"Do you have to be told?" she said. "If so, then writing's no art, and I'm no longer surprised that you were ashamed to call yourself a clerk. Well, I'll do my best. Put into the petition that two lovers are to be laid to rest side by side, and that the one is not to be sent to the anatomy class, so that he will still have all his limbs when the cry resounds: 'Ye dead, ye dead shall all be raised, at Judgment's seat to be appraised!' " Then she again wept bitterly.

I suspected that she was burdened with some great sorrow, but despite her age she gave in to despair only for brief moments. She wept without complaint, and her words were always calm and composed. I begged her once more to tell me the whole reason for her trip to the city. She spoke:

"My grandson, the cavalryman I told you about, was in love with my goddaughter, as I said. He constantly talked about honor to Fair Annie—because of her beauty that's what people called her—and he always told her to be scrupulous about her honor, and about his, too. As a result, soon something quite distinctive became apparent in the girl's features and dress, and she was more refined and better mannered than all other girls of her class. She grew much more sensitive, and if a fellow held her too tightly at a dance or swung her higher than the bridge of the bass viol, she came to me in tears, repeating over and over that her honor had been violated. Oh, Annie has always been a peculiar girl. Sometimes when no one expected it, she seized her apron with both hands, tore it from her body as if it were on fire, and then burst into tears. But there's a reason for that; teeth tore at it; the enemy never rests. I wish that that child had not been so obsessed with honor, had trusted more in our dear Lord and had never left him in her distress and had willingly endured disgrace and contempt in his name, instead of insisting on her worldly honor. The Lord would have had mercy, and will still show mercy. Oh, they'll surely be united. God's will be done!

"Casper the cavalryman was back in France. He did not write for so long that we feared he was dead, and we wept. But he had been in the hospital with a bad wound. When he returned to his company and was promoted to petty officer, he remembered how his stepbrother had insulted him two years before, taunting him that he was only a private and his father a corporal. Then he thought of the story about the French petty officer, and how he had spoken so much about honor when he said goodbye to Annie. He became very restless and homesick, so he said to his captain who asked what was wrong: 'Oh, sir, I feel as if I were being pulled home by the teeth.' As all his officers trusted him, he was granted leave to ride home with his horse for a furlough of three months. He was to return when the cavalry got its fresh horses. He hastened home as fast as he could without harming his horse; since it had been entrusted to him, he took care of it most carefully. One day he felt particularly rushed. It was the day before the one on which his mother had died, and he seemed to see her running along in front of his horse calling: 'Casper, do honor by me!' Oh, on that very day I was sitting at her

grave all alone, wishing that Casper were with me. I had
made a wreath of forget-me-nots and hung it on the sunken
cross. Then I looked down and thought, it's here I'll be
buried, and Casper, too, if God grant him a grave at home, so
we'll all be together when the cry resounds: 'Ye dead, ye
dead shall all be raised, at Judgment's seat to be appraised!'
But Casper didn't come, and I could not have known he was
so near. Still he felt the urgent desire to hurry home, for in
France he'd often thought of this day. He had brought along
a little wreath of golden flowers to decorate his mother's
grave, and a wreath for Annie, which she was to keep for her
day of honor."

Again the old woman was silent and shook her head, but
when I repeated her last words—"which she was to keep for
her day of honor"—she said: "Who knows, perhaps my plea
will be heard yet. Oh, if only I might wake the duke!"

"For what purpose?" I asked. "What do you want from
him, mother?"

Solemnly she stated: "Oh, what would there be to life if it
had no end, what would there be to life if it were not eternal!" Then she continued:

"Casper could have arrived in our village by noon, but that
morning the innkeeper showed him that he had ridden his
horse sore, saying: 'My friend, such a thing does not honor
the rider.' Casper took the reproach very much to heart. He
unsaddled the horse, saw to the wound and continued his
journey on foot, leading the horse by the reins. It was late at
night when he reached a mill only a few miles from our village. Since he knew the miller as an old friend of his father's,
he asked for shelter and received a warm welcome. Casper
led his horse to the stable, put the saddle and his knapsack in
a corner, and then joined the miller in the living room. He
asked for news of his family and was told that I, his old

grandmother, was still alive, and that his father and step-brother were well and prospering. Yesterday they had brought some grain to the mill. The father was now trading in horses and oxen and making a good profit; he also had more regard for honor now and took better care of his appearance. Casper was delighted to hear all this.

"Then he asked about Fair Annie. The miller replied he didn't know her, but if Casper meant the girl who had worked at Rose Manor, he had heard she had taken a position in the capital city, because she could learn more there and more honor came from such service. The miller had heard that a year ago from a garden boy at Rose Manor. Casper was pleased at the news. Though he was sorry he would not see Annie right away, he hoped to find her soon in the city, ele-gant and well-mannered, so that it would prove a real honor for him, a petty officer, to go walking with her on Sundays. Then he told the miller a bit about France, they ate and drank together, Casper helped the miller pour some grain, and finally the miller took his guest upstairs to bed, while he himself slept on some sacks below. The clatter of the mill and his longing for home kept Casper awake, even though he was very tired. In anxious anticipation he thought of his dead mother and of Fair Annie and of how he'd be honored when he arrived home as an officer. Finally he fell into a troubled sleep, disturbed again and again by strange dreams. Several times he saw his dead mother approach him and, wringing her hands, ask him for help. Then he thought he had died, but at his burial he walked along with the others to his own grave with Fair Annie at his side. He was weeping that his comrades did not escort him, and when he got to the church-yard, he found his grave next to his mother's, and Annie's grave was there, too. He gave Annie the wreath he had brought for her and hung the other on his mother's grave, and then he looked around and saw no one there but Annie and me. Then he saw Annie dragged down into her grave by the apron, and he climbed into the grave with her and said: 'Isn't there anyone here who will do me the last honors and shoot into my grave as befits an honest soldier?' Then he pulled out his pistol and shot into his own grave. At the sound of the shot he woke up in great alarm, for it seemed to him that the windows were rattling. He looked around the room, and then he heard another shot and a commotion in the mill and shouts above the clatter. He sprang out of bed and grabbed his sword.

"At that very moment his door opened. In the moonlight he could see two men with sooty faces plunging toward him, swinging clubs. He defended himself and hit one of them on the arm. Then they both fled, bolting the door from the outside as they left. Casper struggled to follow them and finally succeeded in smashing a door panel. He escaped through the opening and ran down the stairs as he heard the miller moaning. He found him lying between the sacks of grain, gagged and beaten. Casper untied him and dashed into the stable to look for his horse and knapsack. Both were gone. In great distress he rushed back to the miller and lamented to him his great misfortune, that all his belongings had been stolen, the horse entrusted to him as well. That the horse was gone drove him nearly out of his mind. Then the miller appeared with a large bag of money he fetched from a closet in the room upstairs. He said to the cavalryman: 'Dear Casper, calm down. You have saved my entire fortune! The thieves were after this bag, which was up in your room, but thanks to the brave defense you put up, I have lost nothing. The men who took your horse and knapsack from the stable must have been lookouts; they fired warning shots when they noticed from your saddle that a cavalryman was at my house. You must not suffer on my account. I shall spare no effort or money to get you back your horse, and if I don't find it, I'll buy you a new one, no matter how much it costs.' Casper said: 'I won't take any presents, for that's against my honor, but if you can lend me seventy thalers in my need, I'll give you a note that I'll pay them back within two years.' On this they agreed, and then the cavalryman hurried off to his village where he reported the matter to a magistrate representing the nobility of the area. The miller stayed behind to await the return of his wife and son, who had gone to a wedding in a neighboring village. Then he would follow Casper and make his own report to the magistrate.

"You can imagine, good sir, with what a heavy heart poor Casper hastened on his way to our village, on foot and poor, when he had expected to ride in proudly; his savings of fifty-one thalers, his officer's patent, his furlough, and the wreaths for Annie and for his mother's grave, all had been stolen. He was near despair when he arrived in his village at one o'clock at night. He wasted no time but went straight to the magistrate's house at the edge of the village, knocked on the door, and, when he was let in, made his report, carefully listing everything that had been stolen from him. The magistrate advised him to go at once to his father, who was the only peasant in the village that kept horses. With him and his brother, Casper could ride around and patrol the area, to see whether he could find any trace of the thieves. In the meantime the magistrate himself would send other people out on foot and await further details from the miller. Now Casper set off for his father's house. On the way he had to pass my little hut, and through the window he heard me singing a hymn; I had been kept awake by thoughts of his dear, dead mother. Tapping on the window, he said: 'Jesus Christ be praised, dear grandmother, Casper is here.' Oh, how the words thrilled me. I hurried to the window, opened it, and kissed and embraced him amidst unending tears. Briefly he told me of his misfortune and of the magistrate's commission to his father, ordering them to set out immediately to look for the thieves. Haste was essential; his honor was at stake that he recover the horse.

"I don't know why, but I shuddered at hearing the word honor. I sensed he would be tried sorely. 'Do your duty, and to God alone be honor!' I said, as Casper rushed away toward Finkel's farm at the other end of the village. When he was gone, I sank to my knees and prayed that God protect him. Oh, I prayed with a fear unknown to me till then, repeating over and over: 'Lord, Thy will be done, on earth as it is in heaven.'

"Driven by a horrible fear, Casper raced toward his father's house. When he climbed in over the garden fence and heard the pump going and horses neighing in the stable, his blood ran cold and he stopped short. There in the moonlight he saw two men washing themselves. He thought his heart would break. One of them muttered: 'The stupid stuff just won't come off,' then the other said: 'Let's go into the stable first so we can crop the horse's tail and cut its mane. Did you bury the knapsack deep enough under the manure?' 'Yes,' said the other. Then they went into the stable. Crazed with distress, poor Casper jumped up and bolted the door behind them, shouting: 'In the name of the duke, surrender! I'll shoot if you resist!' Oh, he had caught his own father and brother as horse thieves. 'My honor, my honor is gone!' he screamed, 'I am the son of a dishonorable thief.' When the two men in the stable heard his words, they were terrified. They screamed: 'Casper, dear Casper! For God's sake, don't cause our ruin! Casper, you'll get everything back! For your dead mother's sake, whose death day is today, have mercy on your father and brother!' But Casper, crazed with despair, could only scream: 'My honor, my duty!' When they tried to break down the door, he shot into the air and screamed: 'Help, help! Thieves! Help!'

"Just then, the peasants roused by the magistrate approached, debating which way they should go to follow the thieves. When they heard the shot and the screams, they ran toward the house. Old Finkel was still pleading that his son should open the door, but Casper persisted: 'I'm a soldier and must serve justice.' When the magistrate and the peasants came toward him, Casper said: 'For the mercy of God, magistrate, my own father, my own brother are the thieves. Oh, I wish I had never been born! I caught them here in the stable, and my knapsack lies buried under the manure.' Then the peasants went into the stable and tied up old Finkel and his son and dragged them into the house. Casper dug up his knapsack and took out the two wreaths, but he did not go into the house; he went to his mother's grave in the church-yard. Day was dawning. I had been out to the meadow to wind two wreaths of forget-me-nots for Casper and me, thinking we would go together to decorate his mother's grave when he returned from his search. Then I heard all sorts of strange noises in the village. Since I don't like commotion and prefer to be alone, I went around the village toward the churchyard. I hear a shot, saw some smoke rising and hurried to the churchyard.

"O Lord, have mercy on him! Casper lay dead on his mother's grave! He had shot himself through the heart; he had fastened the wreath brought for Fair Annie to his coat button and had shot through the wreath into his heart. The wreath for his mother hung on the cross. At the sight I thought the earth would open up beneath me. I threw myself on the dead body, screaming: 'Casper, you unfortunate boy, what have you done! Oh, who acquainted you with your grief! Oh, why did I let you go from me without telling you everything! God, what will your poor father and brother say when they find you like this!' I did not know it was on their account he had done this; I thought it was for a completely different reason. But worse was to come. The magistrate and the peasants brought old Finkel and his son bound hand and foot. Misery choked me, and I could not utter a word. The magistrate asked me if I had seen my grandson, and I pointed to where he lay. Thinking he was weeping on his mother's grave, the magistrate went up to him, shook him, and saw blood gush forth. 'Jesus and Mary!' he cried out. 'Casper's killed himself!' The two prisoners stared at each other in horror. Now Casper's body was lifted and carried along with the group to the magistrate's house. The peasant women helped me to follow, and the entire village resounded with cries of lament. Oh, that was the most sorrowful journey of my life!"

The old woman fell silent once more, and I said to her: "Good mother, your sorrow is great, but God loves you. Those He tries sorely are His dearest children. Tell me now, good mother, why you've come such a long way to submit a petition to the duke."

"Ah, you might now suspect why," she continued calmly, "it's to get an honorable burial for Casper and for Fair Annie. I've brought her this wreath for her day of honor; just look at it; it's soaked with Casper's blood!" Then she pulled a little wreath of gold tinsel out of her bundle and showed it to me. By the faint light of dawn I could see that it was blackened with powder and spattered with blood. My heart ached at the old woman's great distress, and I was awed by the dignity and fortitude with which she endured it. "Oh, good mother," I said, "how will you ever tell poor Annie about all of this without her dying from shock? And what's this day of honor, for which you're bringing Annie the sad little wreath?"

"Dear sir," she replied, "do come along with me now and we'll find her. I can't walk very fast, so we'll get there just in time. On the way I'll tell you about her."

Now she got up and calmly said her morning prayer. Then she smoothed out her clothing and hung her bundle over my arm. It was two in the morning, and day was dawning as we walked through the quiet streets together.

"You see," the old woman continued her story, "when old Finkel and his son were locked up, I had to go with the magistrate to the courtroom. Casper's body was brought in covered with his cavalry coat and put on a table. I had to tell the magistrate what I knew about him and what he had told me at my window that morning. Everything I said he wrote down. Then he looked at the notepad he had found among Casper's belongings; it contained records of expenses, a few stories about honor, including the one about the French petty officer, and at the end there was this notation in pencil." Then the old woman gave me the notepad, and I read what were Casper's last words:

"I, too, cannot outlive my disgrace. My father and my brother are thieves, and they have robbed even me. Though my heart broke I had to capture them and hand them over to justice, for I am a soldier of my prince, and my honor will not allow leniency. For honor's sake I have handed my father and brother over to vengeance. Oh, may all good men plead for me that I be granted an honorable burial here next to my mother, where I have fallen. I ask my grandmother to send the little wreath through which I shot myself to Fair Annie, with my greetings. Oh, I feel her distress from the bottom of my heart, but she should not have to marry the son of a thief, for she has always been proud of her honor. Dear, Fair

Annie, please do not be too shocked by my deed. It could not be helped, and if ever you liked me, do not speak ill of me. My disgrace is not my doing! My whole life I strove to be honorable. I'd already advanced to petty officer and had an excellent reputation in my company, so I'm sure I would have become an officer some day. And Annie, I would never have left you for someone of a higher class—but a thief's son, who for honor's sake had his own father caught and handed over to justice, cannot outlive his disgrace. Annie, dear Annie, please accept the wreath, I have always been faithful to you. God have mercy on me! You now have your freedom again, but do me the honor and never marry someone inferior to me. And if you can, please plead for me that I be granted an honorable burial next to my mother. If you should die in our village, ask that your grave be next to ours. My dear grandmother will lie here, too, then we'll all be together. I have fifty thalers in my knapsack which you should put aside for your first child. The pastor shall have my silver watch, if I am given an honorable burial. My horse, my uniform, and the weapons all belong to the duke, my notepad is for you to keep. Goodbye, my dearest treasure, goodbye, dear grandmother, pray for me, and may you all fare well—God have mercy on me—oh, my despair is great!"

Upon reading these last words of an unquestionably noble and unfortunate man, I was moved to tears. "Casper must have been a really fine man, dear mother," I said to the old woman.

At my words she stopped still, grasped my hand and replied in a trembling voice: "Yes, he was the best person in the world. But he should not have written those last words about despair; they will keep him from getting an honorable burial, and he'll be sent to the anatomy class. Oh, my dear sir, if only you could help me!"

"What do you mean, good mother," I asked, "how can his last words matter so much?"

"Oh yes," she answered, "the magistrate himself told me. An order went out to all courts that only suicides out of melancholy shall get an honorable burial, but all those who killed themselves out of despair shall be sent to the anatomy class for dissection. The magistrate told me that, because of those last words about despair, he'll have to send Casper to the anatomy class."

"That's a strange law," I said, "for if every suicide would come to trial to decide whether it resulted from melancholy or despair, court sessions would last so long that the judge and the lawyers would be brought to melancholy and despair and would themselves be sent to the anatomy class. Be comforted, good mother, our duke is a kind and just ruler; and when he hears the whole story, he'll surely give Casper a place next to his mother."

"May God grant that!" answered the old woman. "You see, dear sir, when the magistrate had recorded everything, he gave me the notepad and the wreath for Fair Annie. That's why I came here yesterday, so that on her day of honor Annie can take the wreath along for comfort. Casper died just in time. If he'd known everything, he'd have gone out of his mind with sadness."

"What's wrong with Fair Annie?" I asked the old woman. "First you say she has only a few hours left, then you mention her day of honor and that she'll gain comfort from your sad news. Tell me everything! Is she to marry someone else, is she dead, or sick? I must know all this so I can set up the petition."

The old woman replied: "Dear sir, I'll tell you; God's will be done! You see, when Casper returned I was not entirely happy, and when Casper shot himself I was not entirely sad. I could not have endured it if God had not had mercy on me and sent me an even greater sorrow. Yes, listen, a stone had been placed before my heart like an icebreaker, and all the sorrows which rushed toward me like chunks of ice and would otherwise have torn my heart to shreds, they all broke apart on this stone and passed me by. Now I'll tell you a sad story.

"When my goddaughter, Fair Annie, lost her mother, a cousin of mine who lived some twenty miles away, I was taking care of the sick woman. She was the widow of a poor farmer. In her youth she had been in love with a hunter, but had rejected him because of his wild ways. The hunter finally sank into such misery that he ended up in prison charged with murder and sentenced to die. This news reached my cousin on her sickbed and grieved her so deeply that from day to day she grew worse. In the last moments before her death, after entrusting Fair Annie to me as my goddaughter, with her parting breath she said to me: 'Dear Anne Margaret, when you go through the town where poor Jürge is in jail, have the prison warder tell him that I implored him on my deathbed to turn back to God and that I prayed for him in my last hour and that I send him my greetings.' Soon after these words my dear cousin died. When she had been buried, I took Fair Annie, who was then three years old, on my arm and set off with her for home.

"Going through the next town on our way, I came to the house of the executioner. As the man was known to have skill in doctoring cattle, our village mayor had asked me to bring back a certain medicine he could prepare. When I went into his house and told him what I wanted, he said I should follow him up to the attic where he kept his medicines and help him choose. I left Annie downstairs in the living room and followed him. When we returned, Annie was standing in front of a small cabinet on the wall and kept saying: 'Grandmother, there's a mouse in there, listen to the rattling, there's a mouse in there!'

"A grave expression came over the executioner's face when he heard the child's words. He opened the cabinet and exclaimed: 'God have mercy on us!'—for he saw his executioner's sword, which hung alone in the cabinet on a nail, sway back and forth. He took down the sword, and I shuddered from fright. 'Good woman,' he said, 'if you are fond of dear little Annie, don't be afraid when I use my sword to make a few slight cuts in the skin all around her neck. You see, the sword moved in her presence and has thus demanded her blood; if I don't cut her neck with it, the child will encounter great misfortune in her life.' Then he seized the child, who began to cry piteously. I, too, cried out and pulled Annie back. Just then the village mayor entered the room; he had come back from the hunt to bring a sick dog to be cured. When he asked the cause of all the outcry, Annie screamed: 'He wants to kill me.' I was beside myself with fear. The executioner told the mayor what had happened. The mayor sharply reproached the man for his superstition, as he called it, and threatened reprisal, but the executioner calmly replied: 'That was the custom of my forefathers, and I'll not change it.' Then the mayor said: 'Master Franz, if you believe your sword moved because I here and now inform you that tomorrow morning you are to behead the hunter Jürge, then I'll forgive you; but it's unreasonable madness to see any connection with this dear little child. Someone could be driven to despair when he finds out later in life that such a thing happened in his youth. No one should be led into temptation.' 'Nor should an executioner's sword,' Master Franz said to himself and hung his sword back in the cabinet. Now the mayor kissed little Annie and gave her a sweet roll from his hunting bag. When he then asked me who I was, where I was from, where I was going, and I told him about my cousin's death and about her message for hunter Jürge, he said: 'You may tell him yourself. I will take you to see him. Though he's quite hardhearted, perhaps he'll be touched in his last hours by the memory of a woman dear to him.' Then the good man led Annie and me to his carriage, which stood before the door, and drove us into town.

"He sent us in to his cook, where we got a good meal, and toward evening he accompanied me to the poor sinner. When I had told the condemned man my cousin's last words, he began to weep bitterly and cried: 'Oh God! If she had become my wife, I would never have ended like this.' Then he asked that the pastor be sent for after all. The mayor promised to carry out his request, praised his change of heart, and asked whether he had one last wish before his death. Then hunter Jürge said: 'Oh, please beg this good old woman to stand at my right side tomorrow, together with her dead cousin's little daughter. That will give me strength in my last hour.' The mayor asked if I were willing, and though I was horrified, I just could not refuse the poor unfortunate man's last wish. He made me give him my hand in pledge, and as I solemnly vowed to come, he sank down on the straw weeping. After that the mayor took me to see his friend, the pastor, who insisted I tell him everything that had happened before he would go off to the prison.

"That night the child and I slept at the mayor's house, and the next morning, heavy at heart, I went on my sad way to the execution of hunter Jürge. I stood next to the mayor in the circle and watched as he broke the staff. Then hunter Jürge said a few words and all the people wept. With great emotion the condemned man looked at me and at little Annie, who stood just in front of me. Then he embraced the executioner Franz, the pastor prayed with him, the blindfold was drawn over his eyes, and he knelt down. The executioner quickly gave him the death blow. 'Jesus, Mary, Joseph!' I screamed, for Jürge's head flew right toward little Annie and set its teeth into the child's apron. She shrieked with fear. I tore off my apron and threw it over the gruesome head. Master Franz rushed over, pulled the head loose and said: 'Mother, mother, what did I tell you yesterday! I know my sword; it's alive!' I was faint with fear, and little Annie would not stop crying. The mayor was extremely upset and had me and the child taken to his house where his wife gave both of us fresh clothing. Later that afternoon the mayor gave us some money, and many townspeople who wanted to see Annie did likewise, so that in the end I received almost twenty thalers and many clothes for her. In the evening the pastor paid a visit and spoke to me for a long time, begging me to bring up Annie in the fear of the Lord and telling me not to worry about all the ominous signs, for they were the snares of Satan and thus to be scorned. Then he gave me a beautiful Bible for Annie, which she has kept to this very day. On the next morning the dear mayor sent his carriage for us to be driven the ten miles to our home. O almighty God! Now everything has come to pass after all!" said the old woman and fell silent.

The old woman's story had made my heart bleed with grief, and I was seized by a horrible premonition. "In the name of God, mother," I cried, "what has become of poor Annie? Is there no help left?"

"She was drawn to it by the teeth," the old woman said. "Today she must die, but despair drove her to it. Honor, honor was all she thought of, the passion for honor caused her disgrace. A man of noble birth seduced her and then abandoned her, and she suffocated the child with the very apron I had thrown over hunter Jürge's head and which she had secretly taken from me. Oh, she was drawn to it by the teeth; she was not in her right mind. Her seducer promised to marry her and told her that Casper had died in France. That filled her with despair and she did the evil deed and then gave herself up to the law. At four o'clock she will be executed. She wrote me to come and see her, and that's what I want to do now. I will bring her the wreath and the greetings from poor Casper and the rose, too, that I was given tonight; all that will comfort her. Oh, dear sir, if only you can manage to convince them with your petition that her body and Casper's, too, may be laid to rest in our churchyard."

"I'll do everything, everything in my power!" I cried. "Right away I'll go to the castle where my friend, the man who gave you the rose, has guard duty tonight. He'll wake up the duke for me, and I'll fall to my knees at his bedside and beg him to pardon Annie."

"Pardon?" replied the old woman coldly. "But she was drawn to it by the teeth. Listen, dear friend, justice is better than pardon. What good is pardon on earth? We all must be judged:

> Ye dead, ye dead shall all be raised,
> At Judgment's seat to be appraised.

You see, she does not seek pardon; it was offered to her if she would name the child's father, but Annie said: 'I murdered his child and I want to die, but he should not suffer. I will bear my punishment to be with my child, but he will be ruined if I name him.' Then she was sentenced to die by the sword. Go now to the duke and beg him to grant Casper and Annie an honorable burial. Go right away! Look, there is the pastor going toward the prison; I'll ask him to take me in

with him. If you hurry, perhaps you'll be able to meet us at
the place of execution with the comforting news that Casper
and Annie will be granted an honorable burial."

While she was speaking we had caught up with the pastor.
When the old woman told him her relationship to the condemned girl, he readily let her go along with him into the jail.
But I ran as never before toward the castle. On the way I was
comforted. It seemed to me like a sign of hope that, as I
passed Count Grossinger's house, I heard through an open
window of the garden house a sweet voice singing to the
accompaniment of a lute:

> Of love did mercy speak,
> Yet honor watches right
> And with much love bids mercy
> An honorable good night.
>
> If love brings gifts of roses,
> The veil let mercy take,
> And honor greets the wooer
> With love for mercy's sake.

Oh, I had still other hopeful signs! After another hundred
paces I found a white veil lying on the street; I picked it up,
and it was full of fragrant roses. With the veil in my hand I
ran on and thought: "O God, that is mercy." When I turned
the corner I saw a man who drew his coat up around him as I
went by and turned his back so I would not recognize him.
He need not have worried, for I saw and thought of nothing
else but mercy, mercy! I dashed through the gate leading to
the castle courtyard. Thank God, I ran into Count Grossinger, who was walking back and forth under the blooming
chestnut trees in front of the guardhouse.

"Dear Count," I cried out with fervor, "you must lead me to the duke at once, on the spot, or it will be too late and all will be lost!"

He seemed embarrassed at this request and said: "What an idea! At this hour? It's not possible. Come back when the duke reviews his troops tomorrow and I'll introduce you."

I felt as if I were standing on glowing coals. "Now or never!" I cried. "You must! A human life is at stake!"

"It's just not possible right now," answered Grossinger with determination, "my honor is at stake. I have been given strict orders not to disturb the duke tonight under any circumstances."

The word honor made me desperate, for I thought of Casper's honor and Annie's honor. I cried: "Honor be cursed. I must see the duke as a last resort in a case where honor has failed. You must announce me or I'll cry out for the duke."

"If you make a move," Grossinger said sharply, "I'll have you thrown into the guardhouse. You're out of your mind, you've no idea of what's proper in circumstances like this."

"Oh, I do have an idea of circumstances, horrible circumstances! I must see the duke, each moment is precious!" I retorted. "If you won't announce me I'll go in alone."

With these words I started out for the steps leading to the duke's rooms when I saw the very same cloaked figure I had previously encountered hurrying toward the steps. Grossinger turned me around with force so that I would not see who it was. "What are you doing, you fool?" he whispered to me, "be quiet, calm down, you'll cause my ruin."

"Why didn't you keep that man from going upstairs?" I asked. "His affair cannot possibly be more urgent than mine. Oh, it's so very urgent, I must see him, I must! The life of an unfortunate, seduced young girl is at stake."

Grossinger answered: "You saw that man go upstairs; if

you ever breathe a word of it, I'll kill you with this sword. Just because *he* went upstairs, *you* can't; the duke has some business with him."

The duke's windows lit up. "God, there's light up there, he is awake!" I cried. "I must speak with him, for Heaven's sake, let me go or I'll scream for help."

Grossinger seized me by the arm and said: "You're drunk, come into the guardhouse. I'm your friend, you'll sleep it off. Then you'll tell me the song that the old woman sang tonight at the doorstep as I came by with the patrol. Her song really interests me."

"It's exactly because of the old woman and her family that I must speak with the duke!" I shouted.

"Because of the old woman?" Grossinger retorted. "Because of her you're making such a fuss? Great men have no time for such things. Hurry, come with me to the guard-house."

He wanted to pull me along when the castle clock struck three-thirty. The sound went right through me like a scream of distress, and I shouted with all my strength up toward the duke's windows:

"Help! For God's sake, help a miserable, seduced young girl!"

In a frenzy of rage Grossinger tried to hold my mouth shut, but I struggled with him. He hit me on the neck, cursed, but I felt and heard nothing. He called for the sentries, the corporal rushed toward us with several soldiers in order to seize me, but at that moment the duke's window opened and a voice called out:

"Count Grossinger, what scandal is this? Bring that man upstairs immediately!"

I did not wait for Grossinger. I dashed up the stairs and sank to my knees before the duke. Annoyed and embarrassed, he told me to get up. He was wearing boots and spurs, but was holding his bathrobe shut around him.

As briefly as I could I told the duke everything I had heard about Casper's suicide and about Fair Annie. I begged him that, if pardon was not possible, he should at least postpone the execution for a few hours and grant the two an honorable burial. "Oh, mercy, mercy!" I cried out, pulling the white veil filled with roses from my vest. "This veil, which I found on my way here, seemed to give promise of mercy."

The duke tore the veil from me, trembling with emotion, and clutched it in his hands. When I uttered the words: "This poor girl is the victim of a false sense of honor, a man of noble birth seduced her and promised her marriage, oh, she is so good that she would rather die than reveal his name"—at these words the duke interrupted me with tears in his eyes, saying: "Enough, please stop, for Heaven's sake, stop!"

He turned to Grossinger who was standing at the door and said urgently: "Away with you! Don't spare the horses! Away to the place of execution! Put the veil on your sword, wave it and shout mercy, mercy! I'll follow you!"

Grossinger took the veil. A complete change had come over him, and from fear and urgency he looked like a ghost. We dashed into the stable, swung up on the horses, and galloped off. He charged out of the gates like a madman. When he put the veil on his sword he cried: "Lord God, my sister!" I did not understand. He stood up in the stirrups, waving and shouting "Mercy, mercy!" We saw the crowd milling around at the place of execution up on the hill. My horse shied at the veil, I'm a bad rider and could not keep up with Grossinger. He galloped on, I made every effort to keep up. Bad luck! The artillery was practicing nearby, and the firing made it impossible for anyone to hear our shouts from the distance. Grossinger was thrown. The crowd drew back. I looked over and saw steel glinting in the morning sun—O God, it was the blow of the executioner!—I galloped up and heard the sobbing of the crowd. "Pardon, pardon!" Grossinger cried and plunged like a madman into the circle, waving the streaming veil, but the executioner held out toward him the bleeding head of Fair Annie, which was smiling at him sorrowfully. Then he screamed: "God have mercy on me!" and sank to the ground onto the corpse. "Kill me, kill me, you people, it was I who seduced her, I am her murderer!"

An avenging fury seized the crowd. The women and girls dashed up, tore him from the corpse, and kicked him. He did not defend himself. The guards could no longer control the crowd. Then the cry went up: "The duke, the duke!"

He drove up in an open carriage; a youth with a hat pulled down over his face and wrapped in a cloak sat next to him. The people dragged Grossinger up to the duke. "Jesus, my brother!" the young officer in the carriage exclaimed in the most feminine tones. The duke, most upset, said: "Keep quiet!" He jumped out of the carriage; the youth wanted to follow, the duke pushed him back not too gently, thereby lifting the disguise. The youth was none other than Grossinger's sister dressed as an officer. The duke ordered the mistreated, bleeding, unconscious Grossinger put into the carriage. Scorning all caution, his sister spread her coat over him. Now everyone could see that she was a woman. The duke was embarrassed but soon regained his composure, commanding that the carriage turn back at once and take the countess and her brother home. This event calmed down the crowd. Then the duke said to the head guard officer in a loud voice:

"Countess Grossinger saw her brother galloping by her house on his way to bring the pardon, and she wanted to be present at the happy event. She was standing at the window when I drove by for the same purpose, and she asked me to take her along in my carriage, something I could not very well refuse the dear girl. She took along a coat and hat of her brother's so she would not attract attention, but because of the unfortunate turn of events her very disguise seemed to hint at a romantic scandal. But, Lieutenant, why could you not protect Count Grossinger from the mob? It's unfortunate he was thrown and arrived too late, but he can't be blamed for that. I want the people who mistreated Count Grossinger arrested and punished."

At these words from the duke, a cry arose in the crowd: "He is a scoundrel, he was the seducer and murderer of Fair Annie, he admitted it, the miserable rotten fellow!"

When the accusations came from all sides and were confirmed by the pastor, the officer, and the officials, the duke was so shaken that he could say nothing but: "Horrible, horrible, oh, the miserable fellow!"

Pale and drawn, the duke stepped into the circle to look at Fair Annie's corpse. She lay on the green grass, clad in a black dress with white bows. The old grandmother, who seemed oblivious to everything going on around her, had placed the head back on the body and covered the gruesome point of separation with her apron. She was occupied with folding Annie's hands around the Bible given her by the pastor in the little town. She bound the little gold wreath on Annie's head and pinned the rose on her breast; it was the very rose that Grossinger had tossed into the old woman's lap, little knowing who she was.

At this sight the duke exclaimed: "Unfortunate Fair Annie! Disgraceful seducer, you arrived too late! Poor old mother, you alone remained faithful to her until death." Now he noticed me standing near him and said: "You told me about a last will of Corporal Casper. Do you have it with you?"

I turned to the old woman: "Poor mother, give me Casper's notepad; his Excellency the duke would like to read his last will."

The old woman, still oblivious to everything around her, said morosely: "Are you back? You should have stayed home. Do you have the petition? Now it's too late, I was not able to comfort the poor child that she would be buried with honor next to Casper. Oh, I lied to her, I said it had been granted, but she didn't believe me."

The duke interrupted: "You did not lie, dear mother. This man did his best, the fall of the horse is to blame. She shall have an honorable burial next to her mother and Casper, who was an honest fellow. They shall both get a funeral sermon on the text: 'To God alone be honor!' Casper shall be buried as a corporal, his squadron shall shoot three times into his grave, and the seducer Grossinger's sword shall be placed on his coffin."

After these words he seized Grossinger's sword, which was still lying on the ground with the veil. Removing the veil, he covered Annie with it and said: "This unfortunate veil that was to bring her mercy shall restore her honor. She has died in honor and pardoned, thus the veil shall be buried with her."

He handed the sword to the commanding officer with the words: "Later today at review you will get my orders concerning the burial of the cavalryman and this poor girl."

Now he read aloud Casper's last words in a voice choked with emotion. The old grandmother clasped his feet, her eyes filled with tears of joy as if she were the happiest woman in the world. He said to her: "Be comforted! You shall have a pension until the end of your days, and a monument shall be erected for your grandson and Annie." Now he ordered the pastor to take the old woman and the coffin, into which

Annie had been placed, to his dwelling, and later escort her back to her home town and arrange the burial. Meanwhile his adjutant had arrived with the horses, so he said to me: "Give my officer your name, I shall call on you. You have shown much human sympathy." The adjutant wrote down my name and bowed graciously.

Then the duke galloped off to town amidst the blessings of the crowd. The corpse of Fair Annie was taken with the dear old grandmother to the pastor's house, and the following evening he drove them back home. The night after that the duke's officer arrived with Grossinger's sword and a squadron of cavalrymen. So Honest Casper was buried next to Fair Annie at his mother's side, with Grossinger's sword on his coffin and his corporal's patent. I was there, too, to escort the old woman, who was filled with childish joy but said little. As the cavalrymen fired their third shot into Casper's grave, she fell back dead in my arms. She was buried with her dear ones. May God grant them all a blessed resurrection!

> On tiptoe they shall humbly go,
> Where the blessed angels sit in row,
> Where God awaits them, newly come
> With a glorious rainbow 'round him spun,
> Their souls will then face God with cheer,
> When at Heaven's gates we do appear!
> Amen.

When I returned to the city I heard that Count Grossinger had died; he had poisoned himself. At my home I found a letter from him which read:

I am very indebted to you. You revealed the disgrace that had long been eating out my heart. I knew the song well that the old woman sang that night, for Annie had often sung it to me. She was an indescribably noble soul. I was a miserable criminal. She had a written pledge of marriage from me and burned it. She worked for an old aunt of mine and often suffered from melancholy. By means of certain medicines with magical properties, I gained power over her soul.

May God have mercy on me! You have saved my sister's honor too. The duke loves her. I was his favorite —the whole tragic story has affected him most deeply —God help me, I've taken poison.

Joseph Count Grossinger

Fair Annie's apron, the one hunter Jürge's head bit into at his beheading, has been preserved in the ducal museum. There are rumors that the duke will elevate Count Grossinger's sister to a princess, with the name *Voile de Grace*, in English, Veil of Mercy, and will marry her. At the next review of troops near D . . ., the monument on the graves of the two unfortunate victims to honor will be erected and dedicated in the churchyard of the village. The duke and the princess will be present. The duke is greatly pleased with the monument; he and the princess are said to have worked out its conception together. The monument represents false honor and true honor, with both figures bowing down deeply on either side of a cross. At one side Justice stands with arched sword, and at the other side Mercy throwing a veil. It is said that in the head of Justice a certain likeness to the duke can be detected, and in the head of Mercy a likeness to the princess.

The Mad Invalid of
Fort Ratonneau

ACHIM VON ARNIM

At home on a cold, stormy October evening, Count Durande, the good old commandant of Marseilles, sat alone by the poorly drawing hearth in his magnificent residence. Shivering, he moved ever closer to the fire, while outside in the street carriages rolled past on their way to a grand ball and in the vestibule his personal valet Basset, who was also his favorite companion, snored loudly. Even in southern France it's not always warm, the old gentleman thought, shaking his head, even here people don't stay young forever, but the lively social life shows as little deference to age as the architecture to winter. What was he, the commandant of the Invalids—such disabled soldiers constituted the garrison of Marseilles and its forts during the Seven Years' War—what was he with his wooden leg to do at a ball when not even the lieutenants in his regiment were any good at dancing? Here at the hearth, however, his wooden leg proved very useful, for he did not want to wake up Basset to push into the fire, little by little, the green olive branches piled up at his side. A fire such as this holds great fascination; the crackling flames seem intertwined with the green branches, and the leaves, half

59

burning, half green, are like hearts in love. At this sight the old man, too, thought of the radiance of youth, and he sank into reveries about the construction of the fireworks displays he had often arranged for the court. He imagined new combinations and ever more complex and variegated wheels and spirals with which he would surprise the people of Marseilles on the king's birthday. At that moment, his head seemed even more vacuous that the ballroom.

In the flush of success, while he envisioned how everything would flash, roar, burst, and then shine in silent radiance, he had shoved more and more olive branches into the fire without noticing that his wooden leg had caught fire and had already burned down by a third. Only now, when he wanted to jump to his feet, with his imagination inflamed and transported by the vision of the grand finale, the firing of a thousand rockets, he finally noticed as he fell back into his overstuffed chair that his wooden leg was shortened and the rest was burning quite alarmingly. Distressed that he could not get up immediately, he used his burning leg to push his chair like a sled into the middle of the room and then called out for his servant and some water.

At this moment a woman rushed up with great ardor to help him. Admitted earlier into the room, she had been trying for quite some time, by coughing modestly, to catch the commandant's attention, but without success. She attempted to put out the flames with her apron, but the glowing embers of the leg set her apron on fire, and now the commandant cried out in real distress for help. Some people soon ran in from the street, and Basset woke up at last. The burning foot, the burning apron made everyone laugh, but with the first bucket of water Basset fetched from the kitchen, the flames were extinguished, and the bystanders withdrew.

The poor woman was soaking wet and could not immediately recover from her fright. The commandant asked for his warm overcoat to put around her and for a glass of strong wine, but the woman refused to accept anything. Lamenting her misfortune, she begged the commandant to let her talk briefly with him in private, so he sent his negligent servant out of the room and sat down next to her.

"Oh, my poor husband," she said in French with a heavy German accent, "my husband will lose his mind when he hears this story. Oh, my poor husband, now the devil will surely play another trick on him!"

The commandant asked about her husband, and the woman replied that it was exactly because of her dear husband that she had come to see him, to bring him a letter from the commanding officer of the Picardy regiment. The commandant put on his glasses, recognized his friend's seal, read the letter and said:

"So you are that Rosalie, with the maiden name Lilie, from Leipzig who married Sergeant Francoeur when he lay as a prisoner of war in Leipzig with a head wound? Tell me about it, it is an unusual love story! Who were your parents? Did they have no objection to the marriage? And from what peculiar eccentricities does your husband suffer because of his head wound that make him unfit for active combat, although he was admired as the best and most capable sergeant, indeed, the very soul of his regiment?"

"Most gracious sir," answered the woman with renewed sadness, "my love must be blamed for everything. It is not that wound, but I who have brought my husband misfortune. My love put the devil in him and tortures him and confuses his mind. Instead of drilling with his soldiers, sometimes he suddenly begins to perform monstrous leaps, inspired by the devil, and commands them to do likewise; or he makes such grotesque faces at them that they shudder from fright, and yet he demands that they remain absolutely motionless at the sight. Recently—and that was really the limit—he threw the commanding general, who had just ordered the regiment to retreat, from his horse, got on it himself and stormed the battery with his regiment."

"A devil of a fellow!" the commandant exclaimed. "If all our commanding generals were possessed by such a devil, we'd need not fear a second defeat like Rossbach. If your love produces such devils, I wish you would love our entire army."

"Alas!" sighed the woman. "It all comes from my mother's curse. I never knew my father. Many men visited my mother at home, and my only task was to wait on them. I was a dreamy girl and paid no attention to the friendly words from these men; my mother protected me from their advances. The war dispersed most of the men who came to see my mother and secretly gambled and played cards with her; we led a lonely life, much to my mother's annoyance. She developed a hatred for both friend and enemy, and I was not allowed to help anyone who went by our house hungry or wounded. That saddened me to the depths of my heart. One day I was alone at home, preparing our noon meal, when many wagons went by filled with wounded soldiers whom I recognized from their language as Frenchmen, captured by the Prussians. I wanted very much to go down to them with the hot meal I'd prepared, but I was afraid of my mother. When I saw Francoeur lying with bandaged head in the last wagon, however, I don't know what came over me; I forgot my mother, took the soup kettle and a ladle and, without even locking our apartment, I hurried after the wagon train all the way to the Pleissenburg. I found my wounded soldier, who had already climbed down, and with great boldness I spoke to those in charge and talked them into giving him the best straw pallet.

When at last he was resting comfortably, oh, what bliss it was to offer the warm soup to the sufferer! His eyes lit up and he swore he could see a halo around my head. I replied that it was my hood which must have gotten turned up in my haste. But he said the halo came from my eyes! Oh, I could not forget his words, and if he had not already won my heart, I would have given it to him for that."

"Those were true words, beautiful words!" the commandant said.

"That was the most glorious hour of my life," Rosalie continued. "I looked at him with more and more ardor, since he said it did him good, and when he finally slipped a little ring on my finger, I felt a richness such as never before. Our quiet bliss was disrupted when my mother arrived, scolding and cursing. I cannot repeat the names she called me, but I was not ashamed for I knew that I was innocent and that he would not believe anything bad about me. She tried to pull me away, but he held me firmly and declared we were engaged, as I was already wearing his ring. How my mother's face changed at these words! It seemed to me as if a flame were burning from her throat, and her eyes turned in until only the whites could be seen. She cursed me and, in a solemn tirade, gave me up to the devil. Just as a bright glow had come into my eyes that morning when I saw Francoeur, now I felt that a black bat had folded its transparent wings over my eyes; the world seemed half shut out and I was no longer my own master. My heart sank in despair, and I had to laugh. 'Do you hear? The devil's already laughing from within you!' my mother said and departed in triumph while I fainted. When I came to, I did not dare go home to her and leave my wounded soldier, who had grown worse from the incident. In my soul I secretly rebelled against my mother, because of the harm she had done the unfortunate man. It was not until the third day that, without telling Francoeur, I slipped home toward evening, but I was afraid to knock. Finally an old woman who had been our servant came out and reported that, after quickly selling all her things, my mother had left town with a stranger who was said to be a gambler, and no one knew where they had gone.

"The whole world had abandoned me, and I felt so happy that at last I could fall into my Francoeur's arms, freed from scruples toward anyone. Since even my girl friends in the city would not recognize me, I could live completely for him and his care. For him I set to work; until then the lace fringes on my dresses had merely served me as play and adornment, but now I was not ashamed to sell these products of my handiwork to bring him comfort and refreshment. When I was not distracted by his lively conversation, however, I always had to think of my mother, who appeared before my mind's eye black with flaming eyes and constantly cursing. I just could not forget this vision. I did not want to tell my Francoeur about it, as it would have burdened his heart, so I complained about headaches I did not have, about toothaches I did not feel, in order to be able to cry when I had to. Oh, if only I had confided more in him at that time, I would not have brought him misfortune! But every time I wanted to tell him that, because of my mother's curse, I felt possessed by the devil, the devil held my mouth shut. I also was afraid he would no longer love me if I told him, and would pick up and leave; even the very thought I could not endure. Such inner torture, perhaps the strenuous work too, finally undermined my health. Violent convulsions, which I kept secret from him, threatened to choke me, and medicine seemed to make them only worse. As soon as Francoeur's wound had healed he made arrangements for our marriage. An aged priest made a solemn speech in which he reminded Francoeur of everything

I had done for him, how I had sacrificed fatherland, wealth, and friendships for his sake and had even accepted my mother's curse; now, admonished the priest, he should assume his share of my burden and together we would endure every misfortune. My husband trembled at those words, but he uttered an audible 'yes' and we were married.

"The first weeks were blissfully happy. I felt relieved of half of my suffering and did not immediately sense that half of the curse had passed over to my husband. Soon, however, he lamented that the priest in his black robes kept appearing before his eyes, hurling threats at him, and he had developed such a violent rage and aversion toward clerics, churches, and saintly images that he felt he had to curse them, without knowing why. To rid himself of such thoughts, he would give in to every whim and would dance and drink, feeling relief only when his blood was coursing rapidly through his veins. I attributed everything to his being a prisoner of war, although I sensed that it was the devil torturing him. Through the efforts of his colonel, who had missed him sorely—for Francoeur is an exceptional soldier—he was exchanged for other prisoners and sent back to his regiment. Light at heart we departed from Leipzig, and in our conversations we imagined for ourselves a glorious future. Hardly had we left the struggle for daily necessities behind us and enjoyed a life of ease at the comfortable winter quarters of the well-supplied army when my husband became more and more nervous and erratic. For hours on end he would pound the drums to distract himself, he quarreled incessantly, and his colonel just could not understand why. But toward me he was as gentle as a lamb.

"I had just given birth to a son when the army set out on a new campaign, and when the pains of birth ceased, I seemed to have been delivered of the devil that had tormented me.

But Francoeur grew ever more capricious and violent. His colonel wrote me that he was daring like a madman, but lucky so far; his comrades thought he had moments of insanity, and his commander feared he would have to be transferred to sick bay or to the Invalids. The colonel respected me and listened to my pleas, until Francoeur's ferocity toward his commanding general, which I've mentioned already, finally led to his arrest. A field surgeon declared that his fits of madness were caused by his head wound, which had not been treated correctly while he was a prisoner, and he would have to spend at least a few years among the Invalids in a warm climate; perhaps this would cure his strange ailment. Francoeur was told only that, as punishment for his offense, he was being transferred to the Invalids, and he left his regiment cursing loudly. I asked the colonel to put everything in writing and decided to confide it to you, so that Francoeur would not be judged according to the severity of the law but according to his misfortune, which my love alone brought upon him; and I hope for his own good that you will assign him to a small, isolated location so that here in the city he won't become the subject of gossip. But sir, a woman who gave you some small help today should be allowed to request your word of honor that you will never reveal the secret of his illness, which he himself does not suspect and which would hurt his pride."

"I'll give you my hand on it," exclaimed the commandant, who had listened to the vivacious woman with sympathy. "What's more, I'll promise to weigh your pleas three times over whenever Francoeur does anything foolish. But it would be better to avoid that, so I'll immediately send him to a fort that requires only three men to command it. There you will find a comfortable apartment for you and your child, and there your husband will have little occasion to do foolish things. If it does happen, no one will know."

The woman thanked the commandant for his kindness, kissed his hand, and he held the lamp for her when she went down the stairs, curtseying many times. This astonished the old servant Basset, and he wondered what had come over his master: had he become romantically attached to the woman on fire, which would diminish his own influence on him? The commandant had the peculiar habit that, whenever he could not go to sleep at night in bed, he would review the day's events out loud, as if he were saying confession to his bed. So while the carriages returning from the ball rolled past and kept the old man awake that night, Basset eaves-dropped in the next room and heard the whole conversation, which seemed all the more important because Francoeur had been his compatriot and, though much younger, his regiment comrade. Basset thought of a monk he knew, who had exorcised the devil in many a case, and made plans to take Francoeur to see him soon. He always enjoyed such ceremonies, so he looked forward with renewed pleasure to seeing a devil exorcised.

Very satisfied with the success of her visit, Rosalie had slept well. The next morning she bought a new apron, put it on, and went to meet her husband, who sang loudly as he led his tired disabled soldiers into the city. He kissed her, lifted her up in the air and said to her:

"You smell like the burning of Troy. I have you again, beautiful Helena!"

Rosalie grew pale and, upon questioning, found it neces-sary to disclose that she had been to see the commandant on account of their living quarters, had found him with his leg on fire, and her apron had burned. Francoeur was annoyed that she had not waited until his arrival, but he forgot his dis-pleasure in a thousand jokes about the burning apron. Then he presented his men to the commandant. He spoke so warmly about their illnesses, handicaps, and spiritual virtues that he won the old man's sympathy, who thought to himself: The woman loves him, but she is German and does not understand the French; a Frenchman always has the devil in him! The commandant asked Francoeur to come in so he could get to know him better and found him well informed about the science of fortification. But he was even more delighted to learn that Francoeur had a real passion for fireworks and had already staged all sorts of displays with his regiment. The old commandant spoke of his own plan for fireworks on the king's birthday, which had absorbed his attention when his leg caught fire the previous day, and Francoeur took up the matter with glowing enthusiasm. Now the old man told him that he and two other Invalids were to relieve the small garrison at Fort Ratonneau, where he would find a large supply of gunpowder, and he and his two soldiers should set to work filling rockets and making pinwheels, sparklers, and firecrackers. When the commandant handed him the inventory and the key to the tower housing the powder magazine, he suddenly remembered what Rosalie had told him, and he detained Francoeur with the words: "But you're not possessed by the devil, are you? You won't cause any trouble?"

"You shouldn't talk of the devil or he'll appear in the mirror," replied Francoeur in a confident tone of voice.

Francoeur's answer renewed the commandant's faith in him. The old man gave him the key, the inventory, and the order to the present garrison to relinquish its command. Francoeur was dismissed. Out in the hall Basset embraced him; they immediately recognized each other and briefly exchanged past adventures. But Francoeur was used to being very strict in all military matters, so he tore himself away, asking Basset, if he were free, to come to Fort Ratonneau the next Sunday to visit its commandant, a position he had the honor to hold.

The move to the fort was a happy occasion for all. The departing garrison had grown tired of the beautiful view of Marseilles, and the newly assigned commanders were delighted with the view, the structure of the fort, the comfortable rooms and beds. From the departing garrison they also bought a few goats, a pair of doves, a dozen chickens, and some devices to trap the wild animals nearby. Idle soldiers are hunters by nature. As soon as Francoeur had taken over the command, he ordered his two soldiers, Brunet and Tessier, to come with him to open the powder magazine, check the inventory, and then take a supply of powder into the laboratory for use in making the fireworks. The inventory proved accurate, and he commanded one of his soldiers to start work on the rockets; with the other Francoeur examined all the cannons and mortar, polishing the brass ones and painting the iron ones black. He also made ready a sufficient number of bombs and grenades and set up all the guns so that the only approach to the fort was covered.

"This fort cannot be taken!" he called out again and again with enthusiasm. "I shall defend my fort even if the English land with a hundred thousand men and storm it! But there was great disorder here!"

"That's the situation in all the forts and batteries," Tessier said. "The old commandant can no longer climb about so well with his wooden leg. And thank God! it has not yet occurred to the English to land."

"That must be changed," exclaimed Francoeur. "I would rather burn my tongue than admit that our enemies could reduce Marseilles to ashes or that we should be afraid of them."

He made his wife help him clean the stone battlements of grass and moss, whitewash them, and then air the food supplies in the ramparts. No one slept much in the first few days, for the tireless Francoeur urged them to work hard, and his skillful hands accomplished more in this short time than others could have in a month. Occupied with such feverish activity, he was undisturbed by moments of madness; he was impatient, but his aims were clear, and Rosalie blessed the day that had brought him to this elevated region where the devil seemed to have no power over him. The wind had turned, and the weather grew so warm and sunny that the summer seemed to be starting anew. Every day ships entered and left the harbor, exchanging salutes with the forts on the shore. Rosalie, who had never seen the sea, thought she had been transported into a new world, and, after so much confinement in coaches and inns, her little son enjoyed the complete freedom of the fort's small enclosed garden; earlier occupants had laid out the garden in a most artistically calculated, mathematical pattern of box hedges in connecting rows, a style liked by soldiers, especially by those in the artillery. Over the fort flew the flag with the lilies: the pride of Francoeur, a joyous symbol for the wife whose maiden name was Lilie, and the child's favorite amusement.

The first Sunday came, blessed by all, and Francoeur asked his wife to prepare a good meal in honor of his friend Basset's visit; his own special request was a fine omelet, since their chickens laid many eggs, and he also brought into the kitchen a number of wild birds that Brunet had shot. During these preparations Basset arrived, quite out of breath but delighted at the transformation of the fort. He inquired in the commandant's name about the fireworks and was surprised to hear that so many rockets and candles were finished. Rosalie now set to work in the kitchen, and the two soldiers left to fetch fruit for the meal; everyone had decided to make the day a special occasion and have Basset read them the newspaper he had brought along. Meanwhile Basset sat in the garden facing

Francoeur and stared at his friend in silence, until Francoeur asked him why.

"I think you look as healthy as ever, and everything you do is so sensible."

"Does anyone doubt it?" Francoeur burst out in rage. "I must know who!"

Basset tried to change the subject, but a frightening change had come over Francoeur; his dark eyes flashed, his head was thrown back, and his lips were pursed. The poor gossip Basset felt his heart sink. In a voice as thin as the sound of a violin he spoke of rumors in the commandant's quarters that Francoeur was possessed by the devil, and he told of his well-meant desire to have him exorcised by a monk, Father Philip, whom he had asked to come up before lunch, using the pretext that mass should be read in the fort's small chapel for the garrison unable to attend church services. Incensed at these words, Francoeur swore he would take bloody revenge on the person spreading such lies about him; he knew nothing of the devil and would not object at all if the devil did not exist, for he had never had the honor of meeting him. Basset insisted he was innocent and had only overheard his master saying to himself that Francoeur had had to leave his regiment because of this devil.

"And who told the commandant about it?" asked Francoeur, trembling all over.

"Your wife," replied Basset, "but she had the best of intentions. She wanted to pardon you in advance if you do anything foolish."

"Divorce!" cried Francoeur and beat his brow, "She has betrayed me, destroyed me, she has secrets with the commandant, she has helped me so much and suffered endlessly, she has made me suffer endlessly, we owe each other nothing, divorce!"

Little by little he seemed to calm down, but within him the turmoil continued; before his eyes he could see the black priest once again, just as someone bitten by a rabid dog feels forever pursued by the image of that dog. At this moment Father Philip entered the garden. Francoeur rushed over to ask him what he wanted, whereupon Father Philip thought the time had come for his incantations and began to address the devil in strong words while he waved his arms crosswise over Francoeur's head. This only intensified Francoeur's rage, and he ordered Father Philip to leave the fort's premises, which he alone commanded. Undaunted, the monk redoubled his invocations against the devil in Francoeur, but when he went as far as to raise his staff, military pride would not permit Francoeur to endure this threat. With furious force he seized little Father Philip by the frock and threw him over the iron gate at the entrance; if the good man's frock had not gotten caught on the spikes of the gate, he would have had a bad fall down the stone steps.

The table was set next to the gate, and Francoeur remembered he was hungry. He called for Rosalie who brought in the meal, her face somewhat flushed from the fire but in very good spirits. She did not notice the monk outside the gate who, barely recovered from his fright, was quietly praying to ward off new danger, and she scarcely heeded how her husband and Basset, the one ominously, the other in embarrassment, stared down at the table. She asked where the two soldiers were, and Francoeur said:

"They can eat later. I'm so hungry I could tear the world to pieces."

Rosalie ladled out the soup, graciously giving Basset the largest portion, and then went back to the kitchen to make the omelet.

"How did the commandant like my wife?" asked Francoeur.

"Very much," answered Basset. "He wished he had been as well treated in prison as you were."

"He shall have her!" replied Francoeur. "She asked about the two absent soldiers, but she did not ask me what's amiss. She tried to win you, the commandant's servant, over to her side by filling your plate to overflowing and giving you the biggest glass of wine. Just wait, she'll also bring you the largest helping of the omelet. If that happens, I'll get up from the table. Then you should take her away and leave me here alone."

Basset was about to reply when Rosalie came back with the omelet which she had already cut into three pieces. She went over to Basset, put a piece on his plate and said:

"You'll never get a better omelet, even at the commandant's. I'm sure you'll have to praise me!"

Francoeur stared gloomily at the platter; the missing portion was almost as big as the remaining two pieces together. He stood up and said:

"Just as I told you. Divorce!"

After these words he marched over to the powder magazine, opened the iron door, went in and locked the door behind him. In complete bewilderment his wife watched him go and suddenly dropped the platter.

"My God, his evil spirit is tormenting him! If only he won't make trouble in the powder magazine!"

"Is that the powder magazine?" cried Basset in alarm. "He'll blow himself up! Save yourself, save your child!"

And he fled, followed by the monk who did not dare to reenter the garden. Rosalie ran into the room where her child lay sleeping, woke it up and lifted it from its cradle, scarcely knowing what she was doing. As unconsciously as she had once followed Francoeur, she fled from him with the child, sighing to herself: "Child, it's for your sake I do this. As for me, I'd rather die with him. Hagar, you never suffered as I

suffer, for I do banish myself!" Lost in her thoughts she went
down the wrong path and found herself standing at the
swampy river bank. Too exhausted to go on, she climbed into
a little boat bobbing in the water at the bank and, pushing off
without difficulty, she drifted downstream. She did not dare to
look back, and whenever she heard a shot at the harbor she
thought the fort had blown up and with it half of her life.
Gradually she sank into a feverish stupor.

Meanwhile the two soldiers approached the fort, laden with
apples and grapes, but Francoeur's strong voice called out to
them as he fired a bullet over their heads: "Get back!" Then
he said through a horn:

"Go to the High Wall, where I'll speak with you. I'm the
sole command here, and I intend to live here alone as long as
it please the devil!"

The soldiers did not understand what he meant, but they
had no choice but to obey their sergeant's orders. They went
down to the steep slope below the fort, called the High Wall,
and they had hardly gotten there when they saw Rosalie's bed
and the child's cradle being lowered on a rope. Their own
beds and belongings followed. Then Francoeur called out
through the horn:

"Take your own things and bring my runaway wife's bed,
cradle, and clothes to the commandant's house; you'll find
her there. Tell her that Satan sends them to her, and this flag
too, to cover up her disgrace and the commandant's."

After these words, he threw down the big French flag that
had flown over the fort. Then he continued:

"I hereby declare war on the commandant. He has time
until evening to arm himself and then I'll open fire. He should
not spare me, for, in the name of the devil, I won't spare him.
Even if he reaches out with all hands he won't capture me.
He gave me the key to the powder magazine, and he can be

sure I'll use it. If he thinks he has caught me, I'll fly with him to heaven and from heaven to hell. It'll be quite a spectacle!"

Brunet finally mustered up enough courage to say:

"Think of our gracious king, who is your sovereign. You won't resist him, will you?"

Francoeur replied:

"The king of all kings on this earth is within me, the devil's within me, and in the name of the devil I tell you to keep silent, otherwise I'll crush you to pieces!"

When they heard this threat, the two soldiers silently gathered up what belonged to them, leaving the rest behind. They knew that masses of rocks had been piled up above them that could crush anything at the foot of the steep stone wall.

When they arrived in Marseilles at the commandant's house, they found him in a state of great agitation, for Basset had already told him what had happened. The commandant sent the two soldiers back to the fort with a wagon so they could save the woman's things from the rain that threatened to fall. He dispatched other soldiers to look for Rosalie and her child, while he met with his officers to discuss the situation with them and plan future strategy. This council of war was particularly concerned that the beautiful fort might be blown up and lost. Soon a delegate from the city arrived to report that the news about events at the fort had spread and that most people believed the destruction of the most beautiful part of the city to be unavoidable. Everyone agreed that force should not be used; no honor could be won in attacking a single adversary, and clemency might avoid a horrible loss. Sleep would finally overcome Francoeur's rage, and when he was asleep, determined soldiers could climb up to the fort and bind him securely. That decision had hardly been made when the two soldiers returned with Rosalie's bed and other things. They brought a message from Francoeur: the devil had revealed to him that they wanted to capture him while he slept, so he, Francoeur, was warning them, for the sake of the poor devils who were to participate, that he would sleep peacefully in the powder magazine, armed with loaded rifles, and, before anyone had the chance to break down the door, he would awaken and blow up the fort with a shot into the powder kegs.

"He is right," the commandant said, "he's not able to act otherwise. We'll have to starve him out."

"He has the winter rations for all of us stored up there," remarked Brunet. "We'll have to wait at least six months. He also declared that the ships supplying the city, which pass beneath the fort, should pay him generous tribute or else he would sink them to the bottom. As a signal that no one should travel at night without his permission, every evening he'll shoot a few bullets over the river."

"It's true! He's shooting!" cried one of the officers, and everyone rushed to a window on the top floor.

What a sight! From all corners of the fort the cannons opened their fiery jaws, bullets whizzed through the air, in the city the crowd took cover amidst cries of alarm, and only a few tried to prove their courage by staying on the street to watch the dangerous spectacle. They were richly rewarded, for with radiant brilliance Francoeur shot a volley of rockets into the air from a howitzer, sent out flares from a mortar, and set off countless fireworks from his other weapons. The commandant pronounced the display magnificent: he himself had never dared to set off fireworks from mortars, but this new technique meant progress for the art of fireworks, which thereby became meteoric, so to speak, and for this achievement alone Francoeur deserved to be pardoned.

The nocturnal illumination had another consequence that no one foresaw: it saved the life of Rosalie and her child.

Both had fallen asleep from the gentle rocking of the boat, and in a dream Rosalie saw her mother, lit up and consumed by internal flames, and she asked her why she suffered so. Then she thought she heard a loud voice shouting into her ear: "My curse burns me up as it does you, and if you cannot break the curse, I remain prey to all evil."

She wanted to say more, but with a start of alarm Rosalie woke up, saw the flares in their brilliance over her head, and heard a boatman right next to her call out: "Steer to the left or we'll capsize a boat carrying a woman with a child."

She saw the prow of a large river boat speeding toward her from behind, like the open jaws of a whale; it veered to the left, but her boat was still tossed sideways.

"Help my poor child!" she cried, and with a hook at the end of a long pole someone caught hold of her boat and pulled it alongside of the larger boat which then dropped anchor.

"Without the fireworks sent up over Fort Ratonneau," one boatman exclaimed, "I would not have seen you, and unintentionally we would have sailed right into you. Why are you out on the water so late, and alone? Why didn't you cry out?"

Rosalie quickly answered the questions and begged them to take her to the commandant's house. Overwhelmed with compassion, the boatman sent his son along to guide her.

There was great commotion at the commandant's house when she arrived. She reminded the old gentleman of his promise to forgive her husband for three blunders. He denied he had meant blunders of this kind; they had spoken earlier of whims and pranks, but this matter was devilishly serious.

"Then it is you who are unjust," Rosalie replied calmly, for she no longer felt abandoned by fate. "I told you all about the poor man's condition, and you still gave him such a dangerous post. You promised to keep our secret, yet you told

everything to Basset, your servant, whose indiscretion and
foolish meddling plunged us into this misfortune. Not my
poor husband, but you are to blame for this misfortune, and
you will have to account for it to the king."

In his defense the commandant insisted he had never told
anything to Basset, and the servant admitted he had eaves-
dropped while his master talked to himself, so the guilt was
his alone to bear. The old commandant declared that he
would have himself shot to death in front of the fort the very
next day, to atone with his life for his guilt toward the king,
but Rosalie begged him not to act rashly; he should recall
how once before she had saved him from fire. She was given
a room in the commandant's house, and while she put her
child to bed, she thought over her situation and in fervent
prayer beseeched God to tell her how she might save her
mother from the flames and her husband from the curse. Still
on her knees, she sank into a deep sleep, and when she woke
up the next morning she could not recall any dream, nor any
divine inspiration. The commandant, who had attempted to
take the fort early that morning, had just returned, greatly
discouraged. He had not lost any men, but Francoeur had
sent so many bullets whizzing to their left and their right and
over their heads, and with such skill, that they owed their
lives solely to his willingness to spare them. He had blocked
the river with his signal shots, and no one dared to travel the
road either, so that traffic in the city that day had come to a
standstill. The city threatened to mobilize its citizens and
come to its own terms with the Invalid if the commandant
intended to renounce all precaution and besiege him as if he
were in enemy territory.

The commandant held back his troops for three days;
every evening was lit up with a magnificent display of fireworks, every evening Rosalie reminded him of his promise of

clemency. On the third evening he told her they would storm the next day at noon; the city had capitulated because all traffic had been halted and its food supplies were running out. He would lead the attack at the entrance, while others would secretly scale the wall from the other side; this way they might surprise Francoeur from behind before he could run to the powder magazine. Lives would be lost, and the outcome was uncertain, but the commandant could not forever endure the reproach that, because of his cowardice, he had encouraged a madman to think he could defy an entire city; he would rather suffer the greatest misfortune than this suspicion. He had settled his affairs before God and the world, and Rosalie and her child were mentioned in his will. Rosalie fell to his feet and asked what the fate of her husband would be if he were caught when they stormed the fort. The commandant averted his eyes and said quietly:

"Certain death. No court martial would recognize insanity as a motive, for his actions show too much intelligence, foresight, and prudence. The devil cannot be brought to court, so Francoeur will have to suffer in his stead."

Rosalie burst into tears, but soon she calmed down to ask whether his offense would be pardoned as a fit of madness if she could get the fort back into the commandant's power without bloodshed and without danger.

"Yes, I give you my word he'd be pardoned!" the commandant exclaimed. "But it is in vain for you to try, as he hates you more than anyone else. Yesterday he called out to one of our sentries that he would surrender the fort if we send him his wife's head."

"I know him," Rosalie said. "I'll exorcise the devil in him, I'll try to bring him peace. If he dies, I'll die with him, so I can only gain if I die by the hand of the man to whom I am married by the most sacred vow."

The commandant begged her to reconsider. He questioned her intentions, but could not oppose either her pleas or her hope of avoiding certain destruction.

Father Philip appeared at the house to report that crazy Francoeur had just hung out a large white flag with the devil painted on it, but the commandant refused to listen to his news, ordering him instead to go in to Rosalie, who wanted to say confession. After she had confessed with the tranquillity of a soul devoted to God, she asked Father Philip to accompany her as far as a safe stone wall where no bullet could reach him; there she would entrust her child to him and money for its upbringing, but she could not yet bear to part with her child. The monk promised with much hesitation to go along, and only after he had inquired in the house if he really would be safe from shots at the designated spot, for he had completely lost faith in his power to exorcise devils, and he admitted that what he had exorcised until then had probably not been the real devil, but some lesser spirit.

Still weeping, Rosalie dressed her child in white with red ribbons, took it in her arms, and went silently down the stairs. The commandant stood at the bottom, and he could barely shake her hand before he had to turn away, for he was ashamed to show his tears to the bystanders. Then she went out onto the street. No one knew what she intended to do. Father Philip lagged behind because he would rather have been excused from going along, and the crowd of idle bystanders followed him, eager to know what was going on. Many people cursed Rosalie as Francoeur's wife, but she did not hear their taunts.

Meanwhile the commandant led his men on secret pathways to the positions from which they were to storm the fort if Rosalie could not rid her husband of his madness.

At the city gates the crowd stopped following Rosalie, for

Francoeur shot in that direction from time to time. Father
Philip, complaining he was tired and weak, said he would
have to rest. Rosalie expressed her regrets and showed him
the stone wall where she wanted to nurse her child once
more; then she would leave it lying there wrapped in her
coat, where it could be found and would lie in safety if she
could not return to it. Father Philip sat down in the shelter of
a rock and prayed, and with firm steps Rosalie went up to the
stone wall where she nursed her child, blessed it, wrapped it in
her coat and lulled it to sleep. Then she left it with a sigh that
dispersed all the clouds within her so that blue skies and the
comforting image of the sun shone on her in radiance.

As she emerged from behind the stone wall and could
finally be seen by her terrible husband, a brilliant light flared
at the gate; she felt a pressure that almost knocked her
down; a blast of air hit her with a roaring noise, and she
knew she had barely escaped death. But all fear had left her,
for an inner voice told her that whatever survived this day
would not perish. Her heart quickened with deep love for her
husband and child when she saw her husband up on the battlements loading his guns and heard her child crying behind
her. The plight of her loved ones caused her more grief than
her own misfortune, and her difficult mission was not the
heaviest burden on her heart. A new shot deafened her ears
and blasted gravel in her face, but she prayed and looked
toward the heavens. Now she entered the narrow passage
between the rocks that was like a lengthened barrel for two
cannons loaded with shrapnel and was designed to aim the
force of destructive shots most efficiently at intruders.

"What are you looking at, wife?" Francoeur bellowed.
"Don't look up, your angels will not come, your devil and
your death await you here!"

"Neither death nor devil can keep us apart any more," she

replied calmly and continued her climb up the massive steps.

"Wife," he cried, "you have more courage than the devil, but it will not help you!"

He blew on the fuse that was about to go out. Glistening sweat ran down his brow and cheeks, and two opposing natures seemed to be fighting violently within him. Rosalie did not want to hinder this struggle, nor impede the passing of time in which she began to have faith. She advanced no further, but knelt down three steps away from the point where the cannon fire crossed. Francoeur tore open his jacket and vest to give himself air; he ran his fingers through his black hair that stuck out in wild ringlets and began to pull it out in his rage. From the force of the blows he aimed at his forehead, the wound on his head opened; his tears and his blood put out the burning fuse, and a gust of wind blew the powder from the touchholes of the cannons and ripped the devil's flag from the tower.

"The chimney sweep liberates himself, he bursts forth from the chimney!" he cried, covering his eyes. Then he paused, opened the gate, staggered down to his wife, lifted her up, kissed her, and finally said:

"The black miner has struggled free, light shines once more in my head, air passes through, and love shall rekindle a fire so we'll no longer be cold. O God, what crimes I've committed in these few days! Let us not rejoice, for they won't grant me but a few last hours. Where is my child? I must kiss it while I'm still free. What does it mean to die? Did I not die once before when you left me? Now you've returned, and your return gives me more than your leaving could take from me: an infinite feeling for life, whose moments suffice in themselves. Now I could live happily with you, though your guilt be still greater than my despair. But I know martial law, and now, God be praised, I can die in my right mind as a penitent Christian."

Rosalie, almost choked by tears of joy, could hardly manage to say that *he* would be pardoned, *she* was innocent, and their child was close by. She quickly bandaged his wound and then led him down the steps to the stone wall where she had left the child. There she found Father Philip, who had gradually crept over behind the rocks to the child. The baby let something fall from its arms as it stretched them out toward its father. And while all three embraced each other, Father Philip told how a pair of doves had flown down from the castle and had played gently with the child, letting it touch them and appearing to comfort it in its solitude. It was when he saw them that he dared to approach the child.

"They were my child's playmates at the fort, and, like good angels, came back faithfully. Surely they'll return and won't leave it."

And, in fact, the doves flew friendly circles around them, carrying green leaves in their beaks.

"Sin has finally left us," Francoeur said. "Never again will I denounce peace, peace benefits me so!"

Meanwhile, after seeing the happy outcome through his field glasses, the commandant approached with his officers. Francoeur handed over his sword to the commandant, who announced he would pardon Francoeur because the wound had robbed him of all reason. He ordered a surgeon to examine the wound and bandage it better. Without taking his eyes off his wife and child, Francoeur sat down and calmly let this be done. The surgeon was surprised that he showed no pain; he pulled out a bone chip, which had caused the wound to fester; Francoeur's robust constitution had apparently worked the chip to the surface, steadily and gradually, until external force, the hand of his own despair, had at last broken through the skin. The surgeon declared that without this stroke of luck Francoeur would have been consumed by an incurable madness. He was put in a cart to save his strength, and his

entry into Marseilles among a people who always respected
daring more than goodness resembled a triumphal march.
The women threw laurel wreaths into the cart, and all sought
to catch sight of the proud villain who had dominated so
many thousands of people for three days. But the men
handed wreaths of flowers to Rosalie and her child, praising
her as their liberator and vowing to reward her richly for
having saved their city from destruction.

It is rare that after such a series of days, something still
happens in a single human life that is worth telling about,
although those who found happiness again and were freed
from the curse did not fully comprehend their good fortune
until later, during more tranquil years. The good old commandant treated Francoeur like a son, and although he could
not give him his name, he left him part of his wealth with his
blessings. But Rosalie received some news which touched her
even more deeply. Many years later, a letter arrived from
Prague in which a friend of her mother's reported that for an
entire year, tortured with agonizing pain, her mother had lain
consumed by remorse at having cursed her daughter.
Ardently longing for salvation of body and soul and tired of
herself and the world, she had lived until the day on which
Rosalie's faithfulness and her trust in God had been rewarded.
On that very day, suddenly reassured by an inner light, she
had died peacefully, confessing her faith in the savior.

> *Mercy* breaks the curse of *sin*,
> *Love* drives the *devil* away.

My Cousin's Corner Window

E.T.A. HOFFMANN

MY poor cousin has met with the same fate as the famous Scarron. Just like Scarron, because of a persistent illness my cousin has completely lost the use of his legs, so that, with the help of sturdy crutches and the sinewy arm of a sullen Invalid —a disabled soldier who when needed acts as his nurse and attendant—he must drag himself from his bed into an armchair laden with pillows, and from the armchair back to his bed. There's yet another similarity between my cousin and that Frenchman who, despite the scarcity of his works, made his mark in French literature with a unique brand of wit quite different from ordinary French humor. Just like Scarron my cousin is a writer, just like Scarron he possesses the gift of a peculiarly vivid sense of whimsy and in his singular way pokes scurrilous fun at the world. But it is to the German writer's credit that he never thought it necessary to spice his pungent little dishes with asafetida so he could tickle the palates of his German readers who find such fare hard to digest. He is satisfied with that noble spice which, while it stimulates and incites, also fortifies. People like to read what he writes; it is said to be good and entertaining; I'm no expert in such matters.

I always enjoyed conversations with my cousin, and I felt more at ease listening to him than reading him. But this indomitable inclination to write has brought black doom upon my cousin; the most severe illness could not slow down the rapid wheels of imagination spinning within him, constantly producing something new. That's how it came about that he told me all sorts of charming stories, which, despite the pain he suffered, he had invented. But the path a thought must follow so it can take shape on paper had been blocked by the evil demon of illness. As soon as my cousin wanted to write something down, not only would his fingers fail to obey, but the thought itself would dissolve and vanish. This plunged my cousin into the darkest depths of melancholy.

"Cousin!" he said to me one day in a tone that frightened me, "cousin, I'm done for! I feel like that old painter deranged by madness who sat day after day with a primed canvas stretched on a frame in front of him, praising, to anyone who called on him, the manifold beauties of the magnificent painting he had just completed. I give up, give up the pulsing creative life that emerges from within me shaped in tangible form to befriend the world! My spirit withdraws back into its cell!"

Since that time my cousin would not let me, nor anyone else, catch sight of him. The sullen old Invalid turned us away from the door, grumbling and yapping like a housedog that bites.

It must be said that my cousin lives rather high up in small, cramped rooms. After all, that's the custom among writers and poets. But no matter that the ceiling is low. The imagination takes flight and builds itself a jolly high vault way up into the shining blue heavens. Thus a poet's little garret, like that garden enclosed between four walls and ten square feet in size, does not, to be sure, have much width and length, but always quite a good height. My cousin, however, resides in the most beautiful part of the capital city, right on the great Market Square which is bordered by stately buildings and in the middle of which stands, in all its magnificence, the colossal and brilliantly designed theater. It's a corner house where my cousin lives, and from the window of a small alcove he can see, at a single glance, the entire panorama of the grandiose square.

One day the market was in full swing when, pushing my way through crowds of people, I came down the street where my cousin's corner window can be viewed from afar. I was more than a little surprised when I saw, glowing toward me from the window, the familiar red cap that my cousin used to wear on good days. What's more, when I came closer I noticed my cousin had put on his handsome dressing gown from Warsaw and was smoking his Turkish Sunday pipe! I waved my handkerchief at him and managed to get his attention; he nodded back most graciously. My hopes were rising! Quick as a flash I dashed up the stairs. The Invalid opened the door; his face, which with its wrinkles and folds usually looked like a wet glove, had actually been smoothed out by the sunshine into a tolerable grimace. He said his master was sitting in his armchair and would see me. The room had been cleaned, and tacked to the screen around the bed was a piece of paper on which was written in large letters:

*Et si male nunc, non olim sic erit.**

All signs pointed to reawakened hope, a renewed desire to live. "Well," my cousin called out to me when I entered the alcove, "well, you've finally come again, cousin! Do you

---

* A slightly altered line from Horace, *Odes*, Book 2, X: "Non, si male nunc, et olim sic erit." = "If things are bad now, they will not remain that way."

know I had a real longing to see you? In spite of your not caring a whit for my immortal works, I'm still fond of you, for you're a cheerful fellow and amusable, if not exactly amusing."

At the compliment of my outspoken cousin I felt the blood rush to my face.

"You believe," continued my cousin without heeding my agitation, "undoubtedly you believe I'm getting better, or indeed even recovered from my malady. Nothing of the sort. My legs are unfaithful vassals who've rebelled against the head of their liege lord and also won't have anything to do with the rest of my worthy corpse. That is, I cannot stir from this spot, and I cart myself back and forth most charmingly in this wheelchair, while my old Invalid whistles the most melodious marches from his war years. But this window is my comfort, here life again has shown itself to me in all its colorful variety and again I must yield to the appeal of its ceaseless activity. Come, cousin, and see!"

I sat down facing my cousin on a little stool that just fit into the window seat. The view was strange and surprising indeed. The whole market seemed to be a single crowded mass of people so that one had to believe that an apple tossed into it could never fall to the ground. The greatest variety of colors glowed in the sunshine, in small patches, that is; I had the impression of a large tulip field blown by the wind in rippling waves, and I was forced to admit that the view was very nice, but, after a while, quite tiring, and in excitable people it might cause a slight dizziness resembling the not unpleasant delirium of an impending dream. I thought this was why my cousin got such pleasure from his corner window, and I told him so quite frankly.

My cousin threw up his arms in dismay, and the following conversation ensued.

MY COUSIN: Cousin! Cousin! Now I realize that you've not the slightest spark of writing talent in you. You lack even the first thing necessary for ever following in the footsteps of your worthy lame cousin: namely, an eye that can really see. To you that market offers nothing but the view of a multicolored, bewildering whirl of people moving in aimless activity. Hoho, my friend! To me it reveals the endlessly changing scenery of city life, and my mind, a gallant Callot or modern Chodowiecki, draws one sketch after another, often with rather bold strokes. Stand up, cousin! I want to find out whether I can at least teach you the first fruits of the art of seeing. Just look down at the street right in front of you, here, use my glass. Do you notice the somewhat strangely dressed woman with the large market basket on her arm who is deep in conversation with a brushmaker and seems to be arranging in great haste certain domestic affairs not related to the nourishment of the body?

I: I've focused on her. She has a bright yellow cloth wrapped around her head in the French manner like a turban, and her whole appearance, especially her face, clearly indicates she is French. Probably someone who stayed behind after the last war to feather her nest here.

MY COUSIN: Not a bad guess. I wager that her husband makes a good living at the local branch of some French industry, so that his wife can fill her basket to overflowing with nothing but the best wares. Now she's going into the crowd. Try to follow her course in its digressions, cousin, without losing her from sight; the yellow cloth lights the way.

I: Oh, just watch the burning yellow spot cut through the crowd. Now she's near the church—now she's bargaining for something—now she's gone—oh, dear! I've lost her—no, she's reappeared over there—at the poultry stands—she's holding a plucked goose—she's testing it with expert fingers.

MY COUSIN: Well done, cousin. Focusing your eyes makes you see clearly. But rather than my boring you with attempts to teach you an art that can scarcely be learned, let me call your attention to all sorts of delightful things that emerge before our eyes. Do you notice that woman at the corner who, even though it's not so crowded there, uses both sharp elbows to make room for herself?

I: What an odd figure—a silk hat of the whimsical form-lessness that has always spited fashion, with colorful feathers waving in the breeze—a short silk cloak of a color faded beyond recognition—over that quite a decent shawl—the gauze trim on her yellow cotton dress reaches down to her ankles—bluish gray stockings—laced boots—behind her a strapping young maid with two market baskets, a fishnet, a flour sack. God be with us! I'm amazed at the furious glances the silken lady hurls about. With what rage she plunges into the thickest crowd! Look how she touches everything, vegetables, fruit, meat, etc., how she eyes and feels everything, bargains for everything and buys nothing.

MY COUSIN: I call that woman, who never misses a single market day, the mad housewife. I think she must be the daughter of a wealthy merchant, possibly a successful soap maker, and a little clerk managed, with no small effort, to win her hand plus accessories. Heaven did not grant her beauty and grace, but instead she got the reputation among all her neighbors of being the most domestic, thrifty girl, and, in fact, she is so thrifty, and makes such a horrible fuss about thrift every day from morning to night, that the poor clerk doesn't know which way his head is on and wishes he were miles away. All the clarion stops of buying, ordering, bargaining, and manifold housekeeping needs are pulled out all the time so that the clerk's household is like a chamber in which wound-up clockwork eternally plays a mad symphony composed by the devil himself; about every fourth day she's accompanied by a different maid. *Sapienti sat!* Do you notice —But no, oh, no, the group forming down there deserves to be immortalized by the pencil of a Hogarth. Just see, cousin, over there by the third doorway of the theater!

I: Two old women sitting on footstools—with odds and ends spread out in a flat basket before them—one of them is selling bright scarves and kerchiefs, trinkets calculated to catch the attention of gullible eyes—the other offers an array of blue and gray socks, skeins of knitting wool, etc. They're leaning toward each other—they're whispering into each other's ears—one is drinking some coffee; the other, completely absorbed in the conversation, seems to have forgotten the shot of schnapps she was about to drink; the two creatures are striking indeed! What demonic smiles they have— what odd gestures with their bony arms!

MY COUSIN: Those two women always sit together, and, despite the fact that the difference in their wares does not admit of conflict, of any real competitive jealousy between them, still, until today they've stolen hostile glances at each other and, if I can trust my practice in studying physiognomies, hurled scornful words at each other. Oh! You see, cousin, see, they're really becoming bosom friends. The scarf hawker hands the sock seller some coffee. What does that mean? I know! A few minutes ago a young girl of at most sixteen was there, attracted by the trinkets in their basket. She was pretty as a picture, and her whole appearance and bearing revealed good manners and modesty imposed by poverty. Her fancy was caught by a white scarf with a colorful border, which perhaps she really needed. She bargained for it, and the old woman used all her tricks of clever salesmanship, spreading out the scarf and letting the bright colors glow in the sunshine. They agreed on a price. But when the poor girl counted out the money knotted into her handkerchief, it was not enough. With flushed cheeks and tears in her eyes, the girl went away as quickly as she could, while the old woman laughed in scorn and folded up the scarf to put back in the basket. No doubt she uttered a few fine phrases. But the other old Satan is acquainted with the girl and, to cheer up her disappointed hawking friend, knows how to turn a sad story about the girl's poverty-stricken family into a scandalous chronicle of frivolity and perhaps even crime. The cup of coffee undoubtedly was the reward for a coarse, blatantly slanderous tale.

I: In all of what you conjure up, dear cousin, there's probably not a single word of truth, but, thanks to your vivid portrayal, when I look at those women everything seems so plausible that I have to believe what you say, whether I want to or not.

MY COUSIN: Before we turn our attention away from the theater wall, let's take a look at the amiable plump woman, with cheeks bursting with health, who is sitting in stoic calm on a wicker chair with her hands folded beneath her white apron; spread out on white cloths in front of her she has quite a collection of brightly polished spoons, knives, and forks, faïence porcelain plates and old-fashioned soup tureens, teacups, coffee pots, stockings, and God knows what else, so that her wares, probably acquired at various small auctions, make a true *orbis pictus*. Without batting an eyelash she listens to the prices offered, unconcerned about the outcome; she settles, reaches one of her hands from beneath her apron to receive the money from the buyer, who then must carry off his purchases himself. Now that's a calm, prudent saleswoman who will get somewhere. Four weeks ago her entire stock consisted of about half a dozen fine cotton stockings and the same number of glasses. With every market day her business improves, and, because she never brings a better chair to market and still keeps her hands beneath her apron as always, she proves she has an even temper and thus won't be deceived by luck into becoming arrogant and foolhardy. What a crazy idea comes to me all of a sudden! At this moment I imagine how a malicious little devil, just like the one under the chair of the devoted worshipper in the Hogarth print, crawls out from under our fat market woman's chair and, envious of her luck, treacherously saws away the chair legs. Crash! She falls down in the midst of her glass and porcelain and her business is ruined. That would be a downfall in the true sense of the word.

I: Truthfully, dear cousin! You've already taught me to see better. When I let my eyes roam back and forth in the colorful whirl of the shifting crowd, now and then my attention is caught by young girls—accompanied by cooks in clean starched dresses carrying enormous shiny baskets—who wander through the crowd and bargain for such household needs as the market offers. The fashionable dress of those girls, their bearing, clearly betray that they are at least of patrician birth. Why are they here at the market?

MY COUSIN: That's easy to explain. A few years ago it became fashionable to send even the daughters of high state officials to the market so that they could have first-hand experience in that part of running a household which concerns buying food.

I: That's a laudable custom indeed; beyond its practicality, it cannot but lead to domesticity.

MY COUSIN: Do you think so cousin? I for my part believe the opposite. What purpose can shopping for yourself have but to convince you of the quality of the wares and the real market prices? The appearance and characteristics of good vegetables or good meat, etc., can easily be learned by the

novice housewife in other ways, and saving the extra tips—
which are not saved at all, because the accompanying cook
makes secret arrangements with the merchants anyway—does
not compensate for the possible disadvantages of a visit to the
market. To save a few pennies, I would never want to let my
daughter, jostled among the common people, be exposed to
the danger of hearing smutty remarks or putting up with some
snide comment from a coarse fellow or peasant woman. Furthermore, as concerns certain speculations on the part of love-
sick youths in blue coats astride horses, or on the part of
those in yellow duffle-coats with black collars on foot, the
market is— But look, look cousin! How do you like the girl
walking over from the water pump, together with her elderly
cook? Take my glass, take my glass, cousin!

I: Oh, what a lovely creature, the very image of charm and
graciousness—but she keeps her eyes lowered in modesty—
her every step is timid—wavering—shyly she stays close to
her companion who works her way through the crowd with
great energy—I keep my eyes on her—the cook stops before
the vegetable stands—she bargains—she pulls the dear girl
toward her who very, very quickly with averted eyes takes
money from her purse and hands it over, happy to get away
—thanks to her red shawl, I won't lose sight of her!—they
seem to be looking for something—at last, at last they stop
near a woman selling fine vegetables in dainty baskets—the
lovely girl devotes her full attention to a basket with the very
best cauliflower—the girl chooses one herself, puts it into the
cook's basket—what? How dare she!—the cook calmly takes
the cauliflower out of her basket again, puts it back into the
market woman's basket, chooses another one, and shows, by
violently shaking her head adorned with a heavy square
bonnet, that she heaps reproaches on the poor young girl who
tried for the first time to make an independent choice.

MY COUSIN: How do you imagine the girl feels, forced into domestic chores completely unsuited to her delicate sensibilities? I'm acquainted with the lovely child; she's the daughter of the chief privy financial councilor, a natural creature to whom all pretense is foreign, endowed with true femininity and gifted with the perceptive mind and sense of tact characteristic of women of her type. Hoho, cousin! That's what I'd call a lucky coincidence! A counterpart to her image has just come around the corner. How do you like *that* girl, cousin?

I: Oh, what a pretty slender figure! Young—quick—gazing at the world with impertinent, uninhibited glances—constant sunshine in the heavens—gay music forever in the air—how boldly, how lightheartedly she trips toward the dense crowd —the maid following her with the market basket seems hardly older than her mistress, and there's much cordiality between them—the young miss wears such pretty things, her shawl is in the latest fashion—her hat appropriate to daytime attire, her dress of a most tasteful pattern—everything pretty and correct—oh, no! What do I see, the girl has on white silk shoes! Imagine, worn-out ball slippers at the market! But the longer I watch the girl, the more I'm aware of a certain peculiarity that I can't express in words. True, she seems to shop with diligent care, chooses and chooses, bargains and bargains, speaks, gesticulates, all of this most vivaciously, almost to the point of nervousness; but I have the impression she wants to acquire more than just household needs.

MY COUSIN: Bravo! Bravo, cousin! Your eye is getting keener, I notice. Look, my dear friend, despite her modest dress, the girl's white silk shoes at the market—not to mention her carefree nature—should have told you that the young miss is with the ballet, or in any case the theater. It will soon be apparent what else she wants—ha, just as I said! See, a bit to the right down the street, dear cousin, tell me whom you discover standing apart from the crowd on the sidewalk in front of the hotel?

I: I notice a tall, slender young man in a short yellow duffle-coat with a black collar and steel buttons. He's wearing a small red cap embroidered in silver, and fine black curls, which are almost too luxuriant, well forth from beneath it. The expression on the pale handsome face is distinctly enhanced by the small black moustache on his upper lip. He has a briefcase under his arm—undoubtedly a student on his way to a lecture—but without taking his eyes off the market, he stands rooted to the spot and seems to have forgotten his lecture and everything else around him.

MY COUSIN: You're right, dear cousin. He can think of nothing but our little comedienne. The moment has come; he's approaching the large fruit stand where the most appetizing fruits are piled up, and he seems to be asking about fruits not on hand. A decent meal cannot possibly be a success without fruit for dessert, so our little comedienne must finish her food shopping at the fruit stand. A round red apple roguishly slips out of her little fingers—the yellow man bends down to look for it, picks it up—the little theater sprite curtseys nicely—a conversation begins—consultation and mutual concern in making a rather difficult choice of oranges fully establishes the ties of a relationship surely begun earlier, and a charming rendezvous takes shape that is sure to be repeated and varied in countless ways.

I: Let the son of the muses flirt and choose oranges all he wants; it doesn't interest me, and even less now that down at the corner in front of the theater, where the flower girls are selling their wares, I've just noticed my angel again, the dear daughter of the privy councilor.

MY COUSIN: I don't like to let my eyes fall on those flowers, dear cousin, there's a special reason for that. The girl who usually has the most beautiful display of select carnations, roses, and other, rarer flowers, is quite a pretty, pleasant child striving to cultivate her mind; whenever she's not busy with sales, she eagerly reads books, the uniforms of which show that they belong to the great aesthetic army of Kralowsky's lending library which triumphantly spreads the light of education into the most distant corners of the capital city. A flower girl reading is an irresistible sight for a creative writer. That's why, when I once went past the flower stands long ago—flowers are not only sold on market days—I stopped in surprise when I discovered the flower girl reading. She sat as if in a dense arbor of blooming geraniums and had the book open in her lap with her head propped up in her hand. The hero must have just encountered great danger, or some other important moment in the plot must have arrived, for the girl's cheeks glowed with excitement, her lips trembled, and she seemed oblivious to her surrounding. Cousin, I want to confess frankly a writer's strange weakness. I felt rooted to the spot—I paced back and forth wondering what the girl could be reading. This thought obsessed my soul. The writer's sense of vanity stirred within me and tantalized me with the suspicion that it was one of my own works which just then was transporting the girl into the fantastic world of my dreams. At last I mustered enough courage, went up to her, and asked for the price of a bunch of carnations toward the back of her stand. While the girl fetched the carnations, I said: "What are you reading, my dear child?" and I picked up the open book. God in heaven! It really was a work of mine, called * * * The girl brought the flowers and told me their modest price. Who cared about flowers, carnations? At that moment the girl was a much more valuable public for me than the entire elegant world of the capital. Excited and inflamed by the most precious authorial feelings, I asked with feigned indifference how the girl liked the book. "Oh, my! Dear sir," replied the girl, "it's really great fun. At the beginning you get a bit dizzy in the head, but then it's as if you were sitting right in the middle of it all." To my great astonishment the girl told me the contents of the little tale so clearly and distinctly that I realized she must have read it several times; she repeated that the book was really great fun, sometimes she had to laugh out loud, sometimes she felt like crying; she advised me that if I had not yet read the book I should get it that afternoon from Herr Kralowsky, for she switched books in the afternoon. But then came the biggest blow.

With averted eyes, with a voice comparable in sweetness to honey from Hybla, with the blissful smile of the enraptured author, I whispered: "Here, my sweet angel, here stands the author of the book that has given you such pleasure, here he stands in person before you." Speechless, the girl stared at me, with her eyes wide open and her mouth agape. I thought this was an expression of great amazement, of joyful shock that the sublime genius whose creative powers produced such a work had appeared so suddenly among the geraniums. Perhaps, I mused as the girl's face remained unchanged, perhaps she cannot believe in the lucky coincidence that brought the famous author of * * * to her side. Then I tried in every possible way to convince her of my identity with that author, but it was as if she had turned to stone, and no sound escaped her lips except "Hm—so—but then—how—" Yet why should I describe to you in endless detail the deep humiliation I suffered at that moment. Just imagine, it had never occurred to the girl that the books she read had to be written first. The concept of a writer, a poet, was completely foreign to her, and I really believe that if I had questioned her further she would have revealed the pious childlike belief that God caused books to grow, like mushrooms.

Completely subdued, I again asked for the price of the carnations. Meanwhile another vague idea about producing
books must have occurred to the girl, for when I counted out
the money she asked naively and without hesitation whether I
made all the books in Herr Kralowsky's library. Quick as an
arrow I shot away from there with my carnations.

I: Cousin, cousin, that's what I'd call truly chastised
author's vanity; but while you were telling me your tragic
story, I did not take my eyes off my favorite girl. Only at the
flower stands did the arrogant kitchen demon give her complete freedom of choice. The peevish governess of the kitchen
put the heavy market basket down on the ground and, sometimes folding her plump arms, sometimes putting her hands on
her hips, whenever it was appropriate to the rhetorical expression of her speech, she abandoned herself completely to the indescribable joy of talking with three fellow cooks; and their
conversation, contrary to the Bible, was certainly more than
yes, yes, and no, no. Just look at what a magnificent bouquet
of flowers the dear angel has chosen and which a robust
fellow is carrying for her. What? No, I just can't approve that
while walking she nibbles cherries from the little basket; how
will the fine batiste scarf probably inside the basket take to
the fruit?

MY COUSIN: The youthful appetites of the moment do not
worry about cherry stains, which can be removed with sorrel
and other household remedies. In truly childlike abandon the
dear girl relaxes completely, now that she is liberated from
the hardships of the big bad market. But for quite a while
I've been struck and puzzled by the man standing right now
at the second pump from here, next to the cart where a peasant woman is selling cheap plum butter from a big barrel. To
begin with, dear cousin, admire the woman's skill; armed
with a long wooden spoon, she first takes care of the larger
sales of quarter, half, and whole pounds, and then, with light-

ning speed, she slaps the triple blobs desired by the greedy nibblers into the paper cups, sometimes even fur caps, they hold out for the butter, which they then immediately consume as a hearty mid-morning snack—caviar of the people! Watching the woman skillfully serving the plum butter with the brandished spoon, I remember something I heard in my childhood: a rich peasant's wedding once was so splendid that the magnificent rice pudding, made with a thick layer of cinnamon, sugar, and cloves, was served with a threshing flail. Each honored guest just had to open his mouth wide to get his portion, and thus the whole affair seemed to take place in a land of milk and honey. But cousin, are you keeping your eyes on that man?

I: Indeed, I am! Who in the world could that crazy figure be? A man at least six feet tall and thin as a skeleton, who moreover stands bolt upright with his back tucked in! Under his small, squashed three-cornered hat the beribboned cockade of a pigtail sticks out, below which his hair hangs down his back loose in gentle waves. His very old-fashioned, long gray coat, with buttons from top to bottom, hugs his body without showing a single fold, and now, when he approaches the cart, I notice he's wearing black trousers, black stockings, and enormous tin buckles on his shoes. What might he have in the square chest he carefully carries under his left arm, which almost looks like a peddler's box?

MY COUSIN: You'll find out soon, just watch attentively.

I: Now he's opening the cover of the chest—the sun shines in—light is reflected—the chest has a tin lining—tipping his hat, he bows, almost respectfully, to the plum butter woman. What an unusual, expressive face—fine, thin lips—a nose like a hawk's beak—large black eyes—arched bushy eyebrows—a high forehead—black hair—a heartshaped toupet with stiff little curls over his ears. He hands the chest to the peasant woman on the cart who calmly fills it with plum butter and, nodding amiably to him, gives it back. With a second bow the man leaves—makes his way to the herring vat—he pulls out a drawer in the chest, puts in the few salted herring he's just bought and shuts it again—a third drawer is reserved, as I see, for parsley and other herbs. With long, ceremonious strides he now cuts across the market in various directions until he discovers a table displaying a lavish collection of plucked poultry. Just as elsewhere, here, too, he makes several deep bows before he starts to bargain—for quite some time he talks with the woman, who listens to him with a particularly friendly expression on her face—carefully he puts the chest down on the ground and takes two ducks, which he easily stows away in his large coat pockets. Good heavens! A goose follows—he glances longingly at the turkey—he cannot resist at least stroking it with his second and third fingers; quickly he picks up his chest, bows most courteously to the woman and strides off, forcefully tearing himself away from the tempting object of his desire—he heads straight for the butcher stands—is the man a cook who must prepare a banquet?—he acquires a leg of veal that also goes into his gigantic pockets. Now he's done with his shopping; he goes down Charlotte Street with such strange dignity and bearing that he seems to have been blown in from some foreign land.

MY COUSIN: Often enough I've racked my brains about this exotic figure. What do you think of my theory, cousin? The man is an old drawing teacher who toiled his life away in second-rate schools and perhaps still does. With all sorts of ambitious projects he made a lot of money; he's a miser, suspicious, cynical to the point of disgust, naturally a bachelor —he sacrifices only unto one God—his stomach; his sole pleasure is to eat well, alone in his room, of course; he has no servants, does everything for himself—on market days, as you've seen, he gets what he needs for half a week and, in a tiny kitchen right next to his shabby little room, he cooks his own food which, because a cook always tries to please his master's palate, he then devours with an appetite of perhaps even animal-like greed. You've noticed, dear cousin, how cleverly he has made an old paintbox into a useful market basket.

I: Let's not talk any more about that horrid old man.

MY COUSIN: Why horrid? Such crackpots must also exist, someone wise to the ways of the world once said, and he's right, variety is the spice of life. But if you find the man that unpleasant, dear cousin, I can make up another theory about what he is, does, and is up to. Four Frenchmen, all of them Parisians, a language teacher, a fencing teacher, a dancing teacher, and a pastry cook, came to Berlin in their youth and, as they could hardly fail to do at that time (toward the end of the previous century), they made a good living. Ever since the moment the mail coach brought them together during their trip, the closest bonds of friendship united them; they stayed bosom friends and, as typical old Frenchmen, they spent every evening after work together, indulging in animated conversation during their frugal meal. The dancing teacher had worn out his legs, the fencing teacher's arms had grown weak from age, the language teacher's rivals, who could boast of their knowledge of the very latest Parisian slang, outperformed his best efforts, and the pastry cook's clever creations were surpassed by the younger palate ticklers trained by the most original gastronomic experts in Paris.

But by then each member of the foursome had feathered his nest well. They moved together into a roomy, comfortable, but out-of-the-way apartment, gave up their businesses, and lived together, true to old French custom, happily and free from care, for they all were skillful in avoiding even the worries and problems of those difficult years. Each one of them has his own special task to further the convenience and pleasure of the group. The dancing teacher and the fencing teacher visit their old pupils, retired officers of high rank, chamberlains, court marshals, etc., for they taught none but the best, and they gather news about current events as material for their conversations that must never run out. The language teacher rummages through the used bookstores to find more and more French works in a language approved by the *Académie*. The pastry cook is in charge of the kitchen; he shops by himself as skillfully as he cooks all the meals himself, assisted by an old French porter. Besides him, since a toothless old Frenchwoman, who had worked her way down from French governess to kitchen maid, had died, their servants now include a chubby-faced boy adopted by the four *Orphelins français*.—There goes their little boy blue, carrying a basket filled with rolls on one arm and on the other a basket piled high with salad greens. I've thus instantaneously transformed the horrid, cynical German drawing teacher into an agreeable French pastry cook, and I believe that his appearance and manner fit quite well.

I: This creation does honor to your writing talent, dear cousin. But for the last few minutes my eyes have been blinded by those tall, white-feathered plumes sticking out above the dense crowd of people. At last the person emerges right next to the pump—a tall, slender, rather good-looking woman—her skirt, made of heavy rose-red silk brocade, is brand new—her hat is in the newest fashion, adorned with a beautiful lace veil—white kid gloves. Whatever made it necessary for the elegant lady, who is probably invited to a luncheon, to push her way through the crowds in the market place? What? She, too, is shopping? She stops and gestures to a dirty old woman in rags who hobbles after her with a half-broken market basket, a living image of the misery among the scum of the people. At the corner of the theater the well-dressed lady signals that she wants to give something to the blind soldier begging there at the wall. She struggles to pull the glove from her right hand—heaven help us! A rough, reddened, quite masculine-looking fist appears. But without much searching or choosing, she quickly puts a coin into the blind man's hand, quickly runs to the middle of Charlotte Street and then assumes a majestic promenade pace, proceeding in this manner down Charlotte Street to Linden Boulevard without paying any further attention to her ragged companion.

MY COUSIN: The old woman has put the basket down on the ground so she can rest, and you can see at a glance all the elegant lady's purchases.

I: They're peculiar indeed. A head of cabbage—many potatoes—several apples—a small loaf of bread—some herring wrapped in paper—some sheep's cheese of a not very appetizing color—some liver—a tiny bunch of roses—a pair of slippers—a boot jack. What in the world—

MY COUSIN: Be quiet, cousin, enough about the rose-red woman! Observe carefully that blind man who got some money from the frivolous child of depravity. Is there a more touching image of undeserved human misery and pious resignation in submission to God and fate? Leaning with his back to the wall of the theater, with both withered bony hands propped up on a walking stick extended in front of him so that thoughtless people won't stumble over his feet, with his deathly pale face turned up and his military cap pulled down over his eyes, he stands motionless on the same spot from early morning until the market is over.

I: He's a beggar, though blind war veterans are well provided for.

MY COUSIN: You're very much in error, dear cousin. This poor man works for a woman who sells vegetables and belongs to the lowest category of such merchants, since the better ones have their vegetables driven in on carts. This blind man arrives every morning so loaded down, like a beast of burden, with full vegetable baskets that the weight almost forces him to the ground and he can scarcely keep himself upright with his cane to totter along. The large, robust woman who hires him, or who perhaps needs him only to bring her vegetables to the market, hardly takes the trouble, when his strength is almost exhausted, to grasp him by the arm and lead him to the right spot, namely, to the place where he is now. There she takes the baskets from his back and carries them over by herself, leaving him alone and paying no further attention to him until the market is over, when she again loads him with the baskets, either empty or only partially emptied.

I: It's remarkable that, even if the person's eyes are not shut and even if no other visible flaw reveals the lack of vision, blindness can always be recognized immediately from the characteristically erect position of the blind person's head; this position seems to express a continuous striving to see something in the all-enveloping night.

MY COUSIN: There's no more touching sight for me than when I look at such a blind man who, with upright head, seems to be seeing into the distance. The sun of life has already set for the poor man, but his inner eye strives to view the eternal light shining toward him from the beyond, promising comfort, hope, and everlasting bliss. But I'm becoming too serious. The blind soldier affords me a wealth of observations on every market day. You'll see, dear cousin, how the Berliners vividly demonstrate their generosity when confronted with this poor man. It often happens that whole lines of people go past him, and not a single one neglects to give him something. But what really matters is how the alms are given. Just see, dear cousin, and tell me what you perceive.

I: Three, four, five coarse, robust housemaids are just passing by; their market baskets are packed to overflowing with what seem to be heavy wares so that their sinewy blue-veined arms are almost cut raw; they ought to be in a hurry to get rid of their burden, but nevertheless each one stops for a moment, reaches into the basket, and hands the blind man a coin without even looking at him. This payment is entered on the marketing list as necessary and indispensable. That's the way it should be! There comes a woman whose dress and manner clearly show that she's comfortable and well off—she stops in front of the disabled soldier, pulls out a purse, fingers her money, and seems to find no coin small enough for the act of charity she intends—she calls her cook over—apparently the cook too has run out of the small coin—she has to get change from the vegetable women—at last she has the desired three-cent piece—now she taps on the blind man's hand so that he'll be sure to notice that he is to receive something—he opens his palm flat—the charitable lady presses the coin in his palm and closes his fingers around it so that the splendid gift won't be lost. Why does that charming little girl skip back and forth, gradually getting closer to the blind man? Ha, while flitting past, she slipped a coin into the blind man's hand so quickly that I'm sure no one noticed but me since I have my glass focused on her—it definitely was not a three-cent piece. The jaunty, well-fed man in a brown coat who saunters up to him in measured steps is surely a very rich merchant. He, too, stops before the blind man and involves him in a long conversation, blocking the way for other people and preventing them from giving anything to the blind man; at last, at last he pulls an enormous green wallet from his pocket, laboriously snaps it open and rummages around so forcefully in the money that I think I can hear it jingle from here. *Parturiunt montes!** I do think that the noble philanthropist, carried away by the image of misery, went as far as to give a paultry cent. By the way, I believe that on market days the blind man makes a rather considerable sum of money, and I'm just surprised that he accepts everything without the slightest sign of gratitude; only a barely perceptible movement of his lips, which I think I perceive, indicates he says something that might be thanks—but I can notice even this movement only at times.

MY COUSIN: There you can see the determined expression of complete resignation: what can money mean to him, he cannot use it; only in the hands of someone else whom he must rely on completely does it have any value—I might be mistaken, but it seems to me that the woman whose vegetable baskets he carries is a fatal, evil seven, a mean woman who does not treat the poor man decently, even though she undoubtedly confiscates all the money he receives. Every time she brings back the baskets she scolds the blind man and scolds him more or less forcefully according to whether she has had a good or bad market day. The blind man's deathly pale face, his emaciated body, his ragged clothing suggest that his situation is quite miserable, and an active philanthropist should really investigate this relationship more closely.

I: When I view the market in its entirety, I notice that the flour carts, with awnings set up over them like tents, are such a picturesque sight because they give the eye a point of focus around which the colorful masses fall into distinct groups.

MY COUSIN: I know the exact opposite to the white flour carts and the flour-covered miller's apprentices and miller's

---

* Part of line 139 from Horace, *Ars poetica*: "Parturiunt montes, nascetur ridiculus mus." = "Mountains will labor and the offspring will be a ridiculous mouse."

girls with rosy cheeks, each one of them a *bella molinara*. I'm sorry not to see a charcoal burner's family that used to sell its wares directly opposite my window at the theater and now has been moved to the other side. This family is led by a tall, robust man with an expressive face, prominent features, with energetic, almost violent movements, in short, the very image of the charcoal burners that tend to appear in novels. In fact, if I ever met this man alone in the forest, I would shiver a bit, and at that moment his friendly manner would be most welcome. A marked contrast to this man is the second member of the family, a fellow scarcely four feet tall and strangely deformed, scurrility personified. You know, dear cousin, that there are people with rather strange builds; at first glance you think they are humpbacked, but on closer inspection you're not at all able to say exactly where the hump is.

I: That reminds me of a naive statement by a witty soldier whose trade often confronted him with such tricks of nature and who was offended by the mystery of peculiar builds. "A hump," he said, "the man has a hump, but exactly where the hump is on him, only the devil knows!"

MY COUSIN: Nature intended to make a gigantic figure seven feet tall out of my tiny charcoal burner, for he has colossal hands and feet, almost the largest I've ever seen in my life. This little fellow, dressed in a coat with a big collar and with an odd fur hat on his head, is constantly in motion; with an unpleasant agility he hops and skips back and forth, turns up here and then there, and attempts to play the role of the amiable gentleman, the charmer, the *primo amoroso* of the market. Not a single girl, unless she happens to belong to the upper classes, gets past him without his tripping after her and telling her sweet nothings while gesturing, grimacing, and striking inimitable poses, all of this, to be sure, undoubtedly in the taste of charcoal burners. Sometimes he lets his gallantry go so far that, while talking, he gently puts his arm around the waist of the girl and, hat in hand, he praises her beauty or offers her his cavalier services. Strangely enough, the girls not only put up with it all, but nod to the little monster in a most friendly way and actually seem to enjoy his gallantry. This little fellow is gifted, I'm sure, with a good dose of natural wit, a definite talent for the comical, and the ability to act it out. He's known as the clown, the prankster, the smart aleck in the whole region around the forest where he lives; not a single christening or wedding or dance at the inn or drinking party can be a success without him; people look forward to his pranks and laugh about them all year long. The rest of the charcoal burner's family, since any children or servants are left at home, includes two women of robust build and gloomy, sullen appearance, probably made even more dismal by the coal dust settled in the wrinkles of their faces. By the way, the gentle devotion of a large white spitz, with which the family shares every bit of food eaten during the market, tells me that life in the charcoal burner's hut may well be quite honest and patriarchal. The little fellow has enormous strength, by the way, for which reason the family assigns him the task of carrying the bags of coal into the purchasers' homes. I've often seen him loaded down by the women with about ten large baskets piled high on his back, and he hopped off with them as if he felt no burden at all. Seen from behind, he cut a stranger and weirder figure than you'll ever again encounter. Naturally, not the slightest bit of the worthy little fellow himself could be seen, but only a gigantic coal sack with two feet grown onto it. A fabulous animal, a kind of fantastic kangaroo, seemed to be hopping across the market.

I: Look, just look, cousin, there's a lot of commotion down there at the church. Two vegetable women have gotten into a violent argument, probably about the tiresome question of what's mine and what's yours, and, standing with their hands at their hips, they seem to be hurling fine words at each other. The people crowd closer—a dense circle surrounds the quarrelers—their voices become ever stronger and shriller—and more and more violently they claw at the air with their hands —they get closer and closer to each other—soon they'll start hitting each other—the police show up—what? Suddenly I see a lot of shining helmets between the furious pair—at that moment the two manage to control their rage—the argument is over—without the aid of the police—the women calmly return to their vegetable baskets—the people, who with loud shouts had cheered them on a few times, probably at particularly drastic moments in the argument, gradually wander off.

MY COUSIN: Do you notice, dear cousin, that during the whole long time we've spent here at the window this was the only quarrel that arose at the market, and it was stilled by the people themselves. The people usually end even a serious, more threatening argument by coming between the quarrelers and separating them. On the previous market day, a tall, ragged fellow with an obnoxious, wild appearance stood between the meat stands and the fruit stands and suddenly got into an argument with a passing butcher's apprentice; immediately using the horrible club he had slung over his shoulders like a gun, he aimed a blow at the apprentice which probably would have knocked the poor man down if he had not skillfully avoided the blow and jumped into his stand. There, however, he armed himself with a butcher's cleaver and started after his opponent. All signs indicated that the whole affair would end with someone's getting killed, so that the criminal court would become involved. But the women selling fruit, all of them strong and well nourished, felt it was their duty to put their arms around the butcher's apprentice so lovingly and tightly that he could not move at all; he stood there with his weapon raised high, just as in the solemn speech about coarse Pyrrhus:

> So as a painted tyrant Pyrrhus stood,
> And like a neutral to his will and matter,
> Did nothing.

Meanwhile, by surrounding the first fellow, who seemed to me to be a released convict, other women, brush sellers, bootjack sellers, etc., had given the police time to approach and capture him.

I: So the people really do believe in keeping order, which cannot but be beneficial to everyone.

MY COUSIN: My observations of the market, dear cousin, have generally strengthened my opinion that the people of Berlin have charged remarkably since that unfortunate time when an insolent, presumptuous enemy overran the country and tried in vain to suppress *that* spirit, which soon sprang up again with renewed power like a spring held down with force. In a word: the people's manners have improved; and if you go to the Zelte gardens in the afternoon on a beautiful summer day and observe the parties boarding the ship for Moabit, you'll notice, even among the lowly maids and day laborers, an effort to be courteous that is quite delightful. The same thing has happened to the masses as that which happens to a single individual who has seen many new things, had unusual experiences, and, along with an attitude of *nil admirari*, has gained a certain ease in manners. The people of Berlin used to be coarse and brutal. For example, no stranger could inquire about a street or a house or anything else without getting a coarse or scornful answer, or being tricked by the wrong directions. The Berlin street urchins, who formerly used the slightest excuse, a somewhat conspicuous suit or a ridiculous accident happening to someone, to do the most obnoxious mischief, no longer exist. After all, those cigar boys at the city gates who sell "the Trusty Hamburger *avec du feu*," those scoundrels who end their lives in Spandau or Straussberg prison, or, as one did a while ago, at the gallows, have little in common with the real Berlin street urchins, who were not vagabonds, but usually apprentices and—it's ridiculous to say—in all their godlessness and depravation still had a sense of decency and no lack of droll humor.

I: Oh, dear cousin, let me quickly tell you how such annoying street humor deeply embarrassed me recently. I'm walking at the Brandenburg Gate and am followed by some freight movers from Charlottenburg who offer me a ride in their wagon; one of them, a youth of at most sixteen or seventeen, is so impudent that he grabs hold of my arm with his filthy hand. "Don't you dare touch me!" I lash out at him. "Well, sir," the boy answers very calmly while staring at me with his large blank eyes, "well, sir, why shouldn't I touch you, are you perhaps not honest?"

MY COUSIN: Ha! Ha! That joke is a good one, but originating from the stinking pit of deepest depravation. The witty words of the Berlin fruit women *et al* were formerly world famous, and someone even did them the honor of calling them Shakespearean, in spite of the fact that on closer inspection their energy and originality could primarily be found in the brazen impudence with which they served up the basest filth as spicy dishes. Formerly the market was the arena for quarrels, fights, deceit, and theft, and no honest woman could dare to do her own shopping without exposing herself to the worst of insults. Not only did the hawkers battle against each other and everyone else, some people even set out with the express intention of inciting disorder so they could fish in troubled waters, as, for example, the rascals recruited from all corners of the earth who were in the military regiments at the time. Look, dear cousin, at the pleasant contrast the market now offers, the very image of comfort and moral peace. I know that overanxious perfectionists and overly patriotic ascetics grimly attack the improved manners of the people, believing that with this external polish their natural simplicity is polished away and lost. For my part I am thoroughly and firmly convinced that people who treat both compatriot and foreigner with courtesy, and not with coarseness or scornful disdain, can hardly forfeit character in so doing. With a striking example that proves the truth of my assertion, I would get into trouble with those perfectionists.

The crowd thinned out more and more; the market square became emptier and emptier. Some of the vegetable women packed their baskets on carts that had appeared, others hauled their baskets away themselves—the flour carts drove off—the flower girls trundled the left-over flowers away in large wheelbarrows—the police became more active so as to keep everything, particularly the line of carts, in proper order; this order would not be disturbed, either, if it did not sometimes occur to a schismatic peasant boy to discover his own, new Bering Straits across the square and, finding them, to direct his bold run through the midst of the fruit stands right toward the door of the German church. Then there was much shouting and much discomfort for the too ingenious charioteer.

"Even now," my cousin said, "this market is the faithful image of eternally changing life. Bustling activity, the needs of the moment, brought the masses of people together; within a few moments everything is deserted, the voices that blended in merry confusion have faded away, and every abandoned spot expresses only too vividly the terrible words: It is no more!"

The clock struck one, the morose old Invalid came into the alcove and said with a sullen expression on his face that his master should finally leave the window and eat, otherwise the food on the table would get cold.

"So you have an appetite, dear cousin?" I asked.

"Oh, yes," replied my cousin with a painful smile, "you'll see in a moment."

The Invalid rolled him into the room. The food on the table consisted of a medium-sized soup bowl filled with clear broth, a soft-boiled egg in a mound of salt, and half a roll.

"A single bite more," said my cousin in a soft melancholy voice, squeezing my hand, "the tiniest bit of the leanest meat, gives me the most horrible pains and robs me completely of the courage to live and the last spark of good humor that still flares up at times."

Putting my arms around my cousin's shoulders and drawing him energetically toward me, I pointed to the slip of paper tacked to the screen around the bed.

"Yes, cousin!" he called out in a voice that cut through my soul and filled me with heart-rending melancholy, "yes, cousin:

Et si male nunc, non olim sic erit!"

My poor cousin!